Harry Ada

SLIM

With a new introduction by
ROY KETTLE

VALANCOURT BOOKS

Dedication: For Jools

Slimer by Harry Adam Knight
Originally published in Great Britain by Star in 1983
First published in the United States by Bart Books in 1989
First Valancourt Books edition 2018

Published by Valancourt Books, Richmond, Virginia
http://www.valancourtbooks.com

ISBN 978-1-948405-17-1 (*trade paperback*)

Also available as an electronic book and an audiobook.

All Valancourt Books publications are printed on acid free paper that meets all ANSI standards for archival quality paper.

Cover by M. S. Corley
Set in Dante MT

INTRODUCTION

Quite how John Brosnan and I actually decided to write horror novels together is a bit shrouded in the mists of incipient dementia. However it happened – and I'm fairly sure it happened in the depths of the Sports Bar in Tottenham Court Rd in London's West End – our first offering in 1983 was based on a film script John had written and is the very novel in which this introduction appears.

The back cover of the first edition said: '*On a deserted oil rig lurks the ultimate horror – a genetically-engineered killing machine – and only six people stand between it . . . and you!*' Who '*you!*' was meant to be was never made clear. Possibly the blurb writer expected readers to look over their shoulders in case there was a genetically-engineered killing machine in the local W. H. Smith bookshop. Not only wasn't there one, but there was a noticeable shortage of copies of the book. I asked the manager of our local shop if he was going to order any more, once the single copy I kept moving to the front of the shelves had gone. I was left with no illusions about the likelihood of that ever happening.

But who could fail to be enticed by that blurb? Or by the cover, which was second only to the excellent one on this edition. Or by the title *Slimer* (a working title only, which due to laziness on the part of the authors got onto the published book)? Or by the name of the author, Harry Adam Knight, HAK – a knowing nod by John to our ambitions?

It was a pretty effective horror novel and, in fact, was one of three Harry Adam Knight books made into films – this time *Proteus* in 1995. The film obviously appealed to the guy who liked the 'giant, tentacle-flinging beast at the finale', and who wouldn't? One keen fan spotted that it was 'pretty much beat by beat an accurate retelling of *Slimer.*'

In fact, of course, *Slimer* was pretty much beat by beat an accurate retelling of the script. I did the first draft of the novel, which wasn't too difficult following John's script and then John improved on it. John's script ended up being used for the film and, later, he wrote a sequel which was never filmed.

British self-deprecation aside, it's a good read and a lot of people agree. Plucking quotes almost at random from Internet reviews: 'wonderful and genuinely intriguing horror book, well written and well researched'; 'Very, very good. Knight certainly knows what he's talking about. The "Phoenix" gives the reader a jolt and leaves you with a question "What would happen if man were to create such a monster?" Stirring stuff and not for the faint hearted'; '*Slimer* is one of those rare finds you find in used book stores. You have no clue what you are about to read, and you have low expectations for the novel. I went into *Slimer* expecting just that, instead I got a shock. *Slimer* is great!!' 'A tense, gripping and claustrophobic thriller packed with interesting characters and some truly chilling scenes'.

An interesting side-note is that Shaun Hutson's *Slugs* ('They slime, they ooze, they kill') was published just a little before *Slimer* by the same company, Star Books. *Slugs* got publicised on the front of London buses. (Slug pushing to front of queue: "I was here before him". Bus conductor: "OK, OK, ooze on first?") Whereas *Slimer* was publicised by means of a party at John's drinking club, The Troy, which we paid for ourselves and to which we invited only one journalist who we resolutely avoided speaking to for the whole evening. *Slugs* is in its umpteenth edition. *Slimer* has had one British edition, a French edition which appeared under the somewhat more evocative title *Terreur Déliquescente* in 1986 from the admirably clearly named Gore imprint of Fleuve Noir, and a U. S. edition as *Slimer* in 1989. Though judging from the way other HAK novels were treated, there might well be other editions which we weren't paid for.

John died in 2005 but I know he'd have been as pleased as me to see that *Slimer* has been rediscovered and I hope that you enjoy it as much as other horror fans have before.

ROY KETTLE
August 2018

Prologue

They were stopping it from eating.

When it was stronger they would be powerless against it. It would scare them away as if they were minnows but now it was confused and the spark of violence was dim. It was weak. It needed food. If only it could return to the sea but they wouldn't let it . . .

The problem was that it could not really understand where they were. Sometimes it felt their presence close by and was aware of the power they were exerting over it. But even at these times it could sense their terror. It knew they would be easy prey if only it could *find* them. Yet it never could . . .

It knew instinctively that in this alien environment it could not rely on its senses any more. Everything was different. No longer was it possible to move effortlessly through the fluid medium that also served as an extension of its sensory organs; this simplicity had been replaced by a strange, dry world where it felt heavy and awkward. Sounds didn't carry as well and the light was too bright and harsh.

Why had everything changed, it sometimes wondered. And the fact it was capable of rudimentary curiosity revealed that *it* too had changed. Strange thoughts and images now flickered through its mind where before its consciousness had been untroubled by anything except the urges to eat and mate.

And in spite of all the changes the former urge remained the dominant one, as it had in the sea. The need for food would blot out everything else and it would be seized in a terrible blood lust that would send it stalking through the endless white corridors, images of torn and bloody flesh filling its mind.

But there was no food to be found within them any more. It was all gone. And *they* wouldn't let it go back to the sea where the food was plentiful. But they were getting weaker too. It could feel it. Soon they would be so weak they'd be unable to prevent it from returning to its own world. And there it would overwhelm them completely.

Then it would be free to feed endlessly.

And grow . . .

One

Christ, it's cold! thought Paul Latham. His face was red raw from the wind except for two white patches on either side of his mouth caused by the effort of keeping his jaws clenched together. He wasn't going to let his teeth chatter like those stupid clockwork dentures that Mark had found so funny back on the yacht.

He knew he would have to give in to the weather soon but for the moment it was important to him to be the last to surrender. Four of the other five in the small boat were holding their thin clothes tightly together and pressing hard into the only source of warmth they had – each other. Mark and Chris looked like they were welded into a single, motionless statue, the only sign of movement being Chris's long red hair whipping across the front of Mark's blue plaid shirt. Linda was burrowed against Paul, her face turned from the wind and Rochelle was similarly clinging to Alex.

Alex, like Paul, was playing the stoic. Both sat upright in the dinghy, shirt collars undone, taunting the cold unnecessarily. Paul's eyes never met Alex's, but his peripheral vision was on full alert for any sign of Alex giving in to common sense. And he knew that Alex was waiting for the same sign from him.

It was, Paul realised, a stupid and futile game they were playing. There could be no clear winner, except the weather itself. But at least it kept him occupied and stopped him from sinking into the despair that he knew gripped the other four.

Not that they didn't have good reason for feeling low – they had been adrift now for nearly three days and their meagre supply of food and water had practically run out. At first they had been confident that they would be quickly rescued; the yacht had sunk, after all, in the middle of one of the busiest sections of the North Sea. Mark, whose father's yacht it had been, had said it would only be a matter of hours before they were picked up. But then dawn had broken to reveal a grey mist that hadn't been there the day before. And the mist had stayed ever since, reducing visibility to less than a hundred feet in any direction. On several occasions during the last three days they had heard the sound of a helicopter flying overhead, no doubt on its way to or from one of the many oil rigs in the area, and once they had heard the sound of a ship's fog horn close by, but though they had yelled themselves hoarse they had remained undetected.

The only thing in their favour was the calmness of the sea. True, it was the middle of summer but that was no guarantee of good weather in the North Sea. Yet ever since the yacht had sunk the water had been remarkably calm and even now with this cold wind that had suddenly sprung up there was only a light swell. It was as if the small dinghy had been nailed to a huge, grey board.

He felt Linda shift slightly. She raised her head, put her lips to his ear. 'I need to take another piss,' she whispered.

He felt a stab of annoyance. 'Again? You had one only a few hours ago. Where's it all coming from? All you've had to drink today is a half a cup of water.'

'I can't help it,' she protested, a little louder. 'It must be the cold.'

Paul looked directly at Alex. He was obviously straining to hear what they were saying. Paul whispered, 'Try and hang on for a while longer. It must be late afternoon by now. It should be getting dark soon.'

She sighed. 'Okay, I'll try. But I don't know if I can wait that long.'

Alex was the cause of this exchange. Whenever anyone had

to answer a call of nature over the side of the boat the others all politely looked away. With the exception of Alex. He regarded it as a great joke, particularly when one of the women was involved, even Rochelle. He would leer openly at them and make obscene comments. On the last occasion, when Linda had needed to urinate that morning, Paul had come close to attacking Alex even though he knew that any kind of struggle in the small boat would capsize it. But Linda had succeeded in calming him down just in time.

Alex. Paul hadn't known it was possible to hate another human being so much. Before the trip he hadn't even disliked him. On the contrary, he admired the good looking Mexican-American with his cool, street-wise manner and the impressive stories of doing drug-runs from Columbia to Florida. But then on the voyage to Morocco, living with him in such close proximity for several days, he realised he was an arrogant, unpleasant pain in the arse. And then, when he had made a blatant play for Linda right in front of Paul . . .

Since the sinking of the yacht he'd become even worse. He'd become increasingly belligerent and cruel, goading them all the time and acting like *super-macho man*. It was odd, reflected Paul, how the crisis had affected each of them differently. Mark's reaction had been to retreat behind a screen of nervous jokes while his girlfriend, Chris, had sunk into a cocoon of self-pity. Alex's girl, Rochelle, coped with the situation by becoming a sleep-walker, taking very little interest in what was happening. Paul himself, he knew, had taken on the role of the stoic, level-headed, natural-born leader. He wondered how long he'd be able to maintain the performance.

The only person who hadn't changed was Linda. She was a little more irritable than usual, true, but otherwise she was the same calm, selfless Linda. He squeezed her shoulder, not caring if Alex interpreted the gesture as an attempt to get extra warmth. She held him more tightly and Paul felt a wave of sick guilt sweep through him. It was because of him she was in the mess. She had been against the trip from the start but he wouldn't listen to her. Alex's grandiose scheme for making a certain £200,000 by doing a dope run to Morocco had blinded him. Now they had lost everything – the dope was at the bottom of the North Sea with the yacht, along with the £4,000 that Linda and he had invested in the trip. And now they might even lose their lives . . .

How much longer could they last, he wondered? All of them were fit – well, perhaps not Mark. But none of them were suffering any serious discomfort yet. That wouldn't start until the last of the food and water were gone, which would be tonight. After then? What would get them first? Exposure? Perhaps, if this cold got any worse. After that thirst would be the big problem. Death by starvation was the least likely scenario. There was a fishing line in the dinghy so they could always catch fish. The trouble was he hated fish. The smell, the taste, even the feel of them were loathsome to him. The thought of eating *raw* fish made him want to gag.

'God, I'm hungry,' said Chris in a clear, loud voice.

Her voice had the effect of rousing everyone from their private thoughts. It was as if they were a bunch of robots whose power had suddenly been restored. Alex grinned at her and gripped his crotch. 'I got some meat right here you're welcome to chew on anytime, kid, long as you don't bite too hard.'

Chris flushed and looked away. Mark pretended he hadn't heard what Alex said. 'Don't talk about food, Chrissie,' he told her, 'you'll only make things worse.'

Rochelle groaned and moved slowly as though afraid she might crack. Sleepily, she said, 'Jesus, I'm freezing. What time is it?'

'Almost dinner time,' said Alex. 'We drew straws while you were asleep and you lost, baby. You're *it*. I get the breasts and thighs so unwrap them and we'll get started.'

'Asshole,' said Rochelle and closed her eyes again. Nothing Alex said ever seemed to rattle her. Not for the first time Paul wondered what the hell she saw in the creep.

Alex grinned. 'Okay, so what are we gonna do, guys?' He looked straight at Paul. 'What about you, Action Man? Any clever ideas?'

His laid-back Californian accent couldn't have got further up Paul's nose if it had been pushed in with a stick. He almost sneered openly at Alex. He knew the game he was playing now. He was trying to make Paul look small; trying to take over. Well, they both knew that Paul had established himself as the leader early on and had the backing of the others. Alex was outnumbered.

'Surely *you* have some smart ideas, Rinaldo,' said Paul, his voice annoying him by cracking slightly from dryness.

'I say we start using the paddles again. Just sitting here is dumb.'

'And paddle in which direction? We don't have a compass. It's a waste of time,' said Paul.

'At least we'd keep warm.'

Paul shook his head. 'As soon as you stopped you'd get cold again, and probably a chill too. It would be a waste of energy. We've got to conserve our strength. But you go ahead if you want, Rinaldo. If there's one person I'd like to watch buried at sea it's you . . .'

Linda squeezed his hand in warning. She was right. A comment like that didn't help anyone. He should be trying to keep the situation calm, not stir up trouble.

Alex glared at him through narrowed eyes. 'You think if we just sit here we're going to get rescued, hey? Come on, Action Man, face facts. Nobody's even *looking* for us. Nobody even knows we're *out* here.'

That was true. When the fire had started on the yacht they hadn't radioed for help. How could they, with three-quarters of a ton of dope on board?

Paul said nothing.

Alex went on, 'We could be waiting months out here in this pea-soup for someone to stumble over us. And by that time we'll be providing a buffet meal for the sea-gulls.'

'The mist will clear soon,' said Paul with a conviction he didn't feel.

'Yeah? Can I have that in writing, Action Man?' laughed Alex.

'Look, smart-arse, you're the *man* as far as you're concerned – *you* got us into this, so why don't you get us out of it.'

'I didn't set fire to the goddamned boat,' said Alex and looked at Mark. '*He* did.'

Mark looked hurt. 'Hey, I told you before it wasn't my fault. There must have been a build-up of gasoline fumes down below. Petrol vapour is heavier than air – it collects in the bilges . . .'

'And who went down there to work on the pump with a lighted joint in his mouth?' sneered Alex.

Mark winced. 'My old man is going to kill me. He loved that damned boat.'

'Serves you right, you stupid dork,' said Alex, 'We were *that* close to making a fortune and you blew it for all of us.'

'Leave him alone,' said Chris, 'it was an accident.'

'Yeah, an accident of birth. The guy's a pinhead.'

Paul sighed. He was about to tell them to shut up and stop squabbling but before he could say anything Linda started to rise to her feet beside him. He grabbed her arm and pulled her back down. 'Are you crazy? You'll tip us over.'

'I *saw* something,' she said in a dazed voice. She pointed ahead. 'Out there! There was a break in the mist.'

They all looked in the direction she was pointing. Paul couldn't see anything but the usual grey wall of mist. 'What did you see?'

'I don't know, but it was *big*.'

Then Paul saw it too. A massive shape looming over them; something the size of a city block standing on four giant legs.

'It's an oil rig!' cried Linda.

'Thank God, we're saved!' shouted Chris. The dinghy began to wobble alarmingly as everyone tried to get a better view.

'Hey, you guys, take it easy!' ordered Alex. 'We tip this thing over and it won't matter what's out there.'

'Alex is right,' said Paul, grabbing one of the plastic loops attached to the side of the boat. 'For *once*. Everyone calm down. We're gonna get the paddles out and head towards it nice and easy. In a half an hour from now we'll be sitting down to bacon and eggs and all the coffee we can drink . . .'

As they got closer to the platform Mark saw it was bigger than he'd realised. He had always been impressed by the underside of fly-overs, with the huge sweep of concrete supported on comparatively thin pillars. Staring up at the rig produced a similar sensation.

The platform was about 150 feet above the sea and consisted of five different levels, each one with a separate deck around it connected by a series of gangways and ladders. On the top level he could see four large cranes but dwarfing them were two large towers, one of which, on the corner of the platform, looked like a smaller version of the Blackpool Tower. This was the one he remembered from TV documentaries and commercials that always had a flame burning on the top – to burn off the excess gas, he presumed. But there was no flame on the top of this one.

Nor was there any sound of heavy machinery being used. The rig was completely silent.

Frowning, Mark squinted up at the platform. It had a very uninhabited look to it. He was reminded of an old derelict house he'd sneaked into as a kid for a dare. He knew the house was empty and he'd banged around making a noise to hide his fear. But the racket had disturbed an old tramp who'd been hiding in there. He came yelling out of a bedroom straight at Mark, who'd run screaming from the house and had night-mares about the incident for weeks afterward. Even now the memory of his terror made him shiver.

'It's deserted,' said Linda, echoing his thoughts.

'It can't be,' said Paul.

They had stopped paddling now and were all staring up at the huge structure that was almost overhead. There was not a sign of anyone on the rig.

Paul put his hands up to his mouth and let loose with an ear-splitting yell. 'Hey, up there! Help! Helllpppp....' The others joined in and for the next minute they were all yelling and screaming up at the platform. Then, breathless, they waited for a reaction.

There was none. The only sound came from the waves lapping against the giant cylindrical legs supporting the platform. Mark noticed that the sea was beginning to get a little rougher. Perhaps they had got to the rig just in time.

'It *is* deserted,' said Alex resentfully. 'They must have pumped the field dry and abandoned it.'

'No way,' said Mark. 'Even if the field's not being worked any more there is sure to be someone still up on the thing. A couple of caretakers at least. If you leave a rig empty anyone can just come along and claim salvage rights.'

'Okay, wise guy,' said Alex, 'where are these caretakers of yours?'

Mark shrugged. 'Asleep maybe. How should I know?'

Paul pointed at the sign visible on the nearest side of the platform. 'The Brinkstone Oil Company,' he read aloud. 'Never heard of it.'

'I have,' said Alex. 'It's one of the smaller American outfits. Owned by one guy, I think.'

'We can't just sit here,' said Linda. 'We've got to get *up* there . . .'

'But how?' asked Rochelle, 'you see any escalators?'

She was right. Neither the four supporting legs nor the network of girder struts between them offered any visible means of climbing up to the platform.

'There *has* to be a way to get up there,' said Paul. 'They can't just use helicopters all the time to get on and off. What if they want to transfer people or equipment from boats . . . ?'

Unexpectedly, he got his answer. There was the sound of

an engine suddenly starting up somewhere on the rig and then one of the cranes began to move. In startled silence they watched as the arm of the crane swung out over the top of the platform holding a large metal cage. Then they all started to cheer as they realised what was happening.

The cage was swiftly lowered until it was suspended just above the water a mere ten yards or so from their boat. As quickly as possible they paddled over to it. The cage was about eight feet wide and had only three sides. The fourth side was open, apart from a chain stretched across it.

Getting from the boat into the cage was a tricky manoeuvre and all of them were soaked to the waist by the time they were inside and clinging to the wide steel mesh of the sides.

There was a jerk and the cage began to rise rapidly. Mark watched the life-boat get smaller and smaller as it drifted away. It looked a disturbingly fragile little vessel seen from above in this way and he wondered how much longer they could have survived in it, particularly as the sea was beginning to turn ominous.

The cage continued to rise and Mark felt a wave of dizziness overcome him. He didn't like heights at the best of times. Swallowing hard he shut his eyes and clung tightly to the mesh, hoping the others weren't noticing his distress.

'Now I know what a fish feels like when it's hauled out of the sea in a net,' he heard Linda gasp.

Then came a jarring bump and he opened his eyes. The cage was now sitting safely on the top deck of the platform. Nearby were three huge chimneys and looming overhead was the boom of the crane that had rescued them but there was no sign of any welcoming committee. The place was deserted.

They got shakily out of the cage and stood looking around. After all that time at sea it felt strange to be on something solid again.

'Where *is* everyone?' asked Chris.

Paul was staring up at the driver's cabin on the crane. Sounding puzzled, he said, 'I can't even see anyone inside that thing.'

'There's gotta be!' cried Alex. 'You think it picked us up all by itself?'

'Then where is he?'

'I'll go see,' said Mark suddenly and hurried over to the ladder leading up to the cabin. It wasn't too high and he was anxious to make up for his display of weakness in the cage. While the others watched he began to climb.

Halfway up he knew he'd made a mistake. The familiar dizziness swept over him and he was forced to stop and shut his eyes for a few moments. But then he forced himself to continue on and, to his relief, he finally made it to the open cabin doorway.

He was so thankful to have got up there the fact that the cabin was empty didn't sink in at first. Then, when it did, he stared around the cramped interior with a growing sense of confusion. It was crazy! There was no way the driver could have got down the ladder without them seeing him. So where was he?

Then Mark saw the overalls. They were lying in a corner at the rear of the cabin. Mark frowned as he bent over them for a closer look. There was something strange in the way they were lying there – as if someone had spent time arranging the arms and legs instead of just dropping the garment on the floor.

He picked up one of the sleeves then recoiled with disgust as a black, oily tendril of slime slowly dropped from the cuff onto the metal floor. A horrible smell filled the cabin and Mark started to choke. He knew he had to get out of there and *fast*.

Two

Mark came down the ladder so fast he almost fell. The others hurried over to him and saw that he was white and shaking.

'Mark, what's wrong?' cried Chris, 'what's up there?'

Mark was taking deep breaths, his face screwed up as if he was tasting something awful. 'There's nothing up there,' he gasped finally, 'just a pair of overalls. But they *stink* something horrible . . .'

'Is *that* what all the panic is about?' sneered Alex. 'A pair of smelly overalls?'

'*You* go up and smell them,' said Mark angrily. 'It's like something's been dead and rotting up there for weeks.'

'But you didn't see any sign of the driver?' asked Paul worriedly.

Mark shook his head.

'Then where did he get to? How come we didn't see him come down?' asked Linda.

'Good question,' said Paul, staring around the empty, deserted-looking deck. The wind, as it blew over the tops of the three squat chimneys, made an eerie whistling sound. He shivered. He was beginning to feel cold again. The psychological warmth generated by their rescue was beginning to fade. And he could tell that his companions were experiencing a similar feeling of anxiety. Linda, tall and slim with her dark, tight-curled hair tumbling to her shoulders, was looking like a nervous deer about to bolt towards the nearest cover; Mark and Chris were holding onto each other and Rochelle, edging closer to Alex, looked much younger and more vulnerable than usual. Even Alex wasn't bothering to conceal an obvious nervousness. For some reason Paul found this the most disturbing thing of all.

'Well, guys,' he said with a forced heartiness, 'this isn't

getting us anywhere. Let's get under cover and start looking for our bashful hosts before we freeze to death.'

Alex suddenly snapped his fingers and said, 'Remote control.'

Paul looked at him blankly. 'What?'

'Remote control. That's how they ran that crane routine. I'll bet all the equipment around here can be operated by remote control,' he said triumphantly, sounding like his usual self again. Then he pointed. 'And look. *That's* how they saw us.'

Paul looked in the direction Alex was pointing. He saw what appeared to be a small TV camera attached to a pole near the crane.

'And there's another one!' cried Alex, pointing towards the circular helicopter landing pad that extended out from the far corner of the roof.

Paul nodded. 'You may be right,' he admitted reluctantly. 'But that doesn't explain why they haven't made an appearance yet.'

Alex shrugged. 'Maybe there's only one caretaker on the rig and he's busy or something. How should I know?'

'Come *on*,' said Rochelle, 'let's go find out before my tits fall off from the cold.' The wind was whipping her pink-streaked hair and her lips were almost the same colour as the small blue jewel on the side of her nose. Paul couldn't help glancing down at her nipples which were clearly visible – hard and swollen – behind the thin fabric of her shirt.

He grinned and nodded. 'Yes, you're right. We'll go down to the next deck and see if we can find a way inside.' He gestured towards the top of the ladder that led to the deck below. 'Alex, why don't you and Ro lead the way?'

Alex seemed to be about to argue for a moment but then apparently changed his mind. 'Okay,' he grunted. 'Come on Ro.'

As Alex disappeared from view down the ladder Paul turned to Mark and Chris. 'You go next, Linda and I'll bring up the rear.' But Mark wasn't listening. He was staring up at the empty driver's cabin on the crane. Paul realised he didn't look well. There was a darkness under his eyes and his cheeks seemed sunken. 'Hey, Mark, you in there?'

Mark blinked and looked round at him. Paul didn't like the look of him. In all the years he'd known him Mark had never been particularly healthy but now he was a physical wreck. His weight was down to about nine and a half stone and his skin had a yellowish pallor to it. It wasn't just due to the privations of the last three days; Mark had been losing weight before the shipwreck. Paul had tried to find out what was wrong with him but everytime he brought the subject up Mark had sidestepped it.

'Mark? Are you okay?'

'Huh? Oh, yeah. I'm okay.' He returned his gaze to the crane cabin. 'Paul,' he added quietly, 'There was something *in* the overalls up there.'

Paul frowned. '*In* the overalls? What do you mean?'

'They were full of slime. Black slime. Horrible stuff. That's where the stink was coming from . . .'

Chris was looking at him worriedly now. 'Mark, are you sure you feel okay?'

'What do you think it was?' asked Mark, ignoring her.

'The slime? Probably just grease,' said Paul. 'That's what overalls are for – to get grease on. And this *is* an oil rig after all . . .'

'But *inside*?'

'It probably just soaked through. Mark, why are you making such a big production over a bit of grease?'

'You don't understand,' persisted Mark, shaking his head. 'It wasn't just . . .' At this point he was interrupted by a yell from Alex. 'Hey, you guys! Come on down! We found a way in!'

'Okay! We're coming!' Paul yelled back. Then he turned back to Mark and said, impatiently, 'Well? What were you going to say?'

Mark sighed. 'Forget it. It was nothing. Just my imagination I guess.' He gave the crane one last look then headed for the ladder. Chris hurried after him.

He's definitely close to cracking up, thought Paul sombrely as he followed them.

When he arrived on the catwalk below he saw the others were gathered around an open door looking pleased with themselves. 'Voila!' cried Linda, indicating the doorway with a flourish as he approached.

He looked inside. He found himself staring down a short, featureless corridor that ended with a black, opaque glass door. That's odd, he thought. He didn't really know what he expected to see but it certainly wasn't this.

'Still no sign of any welcoming committee,' he muttered, 'I guess we might as well go in.' He entered the corridor and walked along to the glass door. The others followed him.

There was no handle on the door but there was a red button set in the wall beside it. 'Push it,' said Mark. 'It might be the doorbell.'

Paul pushed it. The door slid silently open – to reveal yet another similar door some six feet away. At the same time a panel in the ceiling began to produce an intense violet light.

'Weird,' said Alex.

Enveloped by the bright, eerie glow from above Paul walked along to the next door. There was another button beside it so he pushed it. Nothing happened.

As the others crowded in behind him Mark said nervously, 'You think this light is safe? I can actually *feel* it on my skin.'

Paul kept pushing the button. 'It's some sort of sterilising device, I think. Though what it's doing on an oil rig is beyond me.'

'Steriliser?' Alex gave a forced laugh. 'Huh, if my balls turn green Brinkstone is gonna hear from my lawyers. Open that damn door, will you . . . ?'

'It won't open,' said Paul helplessly.

'Perhaps we have to close the other one first,' suggested

Linda. She was examining the wall. 'There's another button back here. Shall I give it a go?'

Paul hesitated. He didn't like the idea of being trapped between the two doors, especially with that light shining on them – it was making *his* skin tingle too. But finally he said, 'Yeah. Push it.'

The outer door slid shut behind them. Paul tried the other button again. To his relief the door opened. And the violet light switched off.

Ahead stretched a long, gleaming white corridor illuminated by fluorescent strip lighting. It reminded Paul of a hospital. There was even a strong whiff of disinfectant in the air.

They stared down the corridor in silent wonder. Then Mark said, 'I'm beginning to think this is no ordinary oil rig.'

'Congratulations,' sneered Alex. 'That must have used up a lot of grey cells, dickhead.'

'What *is* this place then?' asked Linda.

'You've got me,' admitted Paul.

Unexpectedly Rochelle let loose a piercing yell that made them all jump. '*Hey! Is anybody home?!*'

Her voice echoed down the corridor then faded away. There was no response.

'Jesus, *warn* me before you do that again, you bitch,' muttered Alex.

'I don't like this,' said Chris worriedly. 'It's creepy. There's something wrong here. I can sense it.'

'We don't need any of your psychic stuff just now, okay?' said Paul, more curtly than he meant to. 'We're all feeling jumpy enough without you having to pile on the agony.' It was one of the things that annoyed him about Chris. If she wasn't going on about ecology, natural food and the industrial rape of the environment she was waffling on about astrology and her psychic powers. She and Mark had spent a month last summer trekking up and down the countryside following the routes of so-called 'ley-lines' which she swore she could *feel*.

She and Mark made a good pair. Both were a bit loony in their way.

'Come on,' he said brusquely, 'let's go find someone who can tell us what all this is about.' He strode off purposefully and knocked loudly on the first door he came to. There was no reply so he tried the handle. The white-painted door opened. He looked inside.

The lights were on and he could tell at a glance that the room was empty. He entered cautiously, feeling something of a trespasser. He kept expecting someone to appear suddenly and angrily demand to know what they were doing there.

It was a big room and obviously a laboratory of some sort. It was filled with all kinds of scientific equipment – microscopes, racks of test tubes, sterilising cabinets, humidifiers, refrigerators and various other things he couldn't identify. The only touch of colour amidst the oppressive whiteness was provided by several wall charts featuring graphs and diagrams, and what appeared to be a piece of abstract sculpture made up of hundreds of garishly painted ping pong balls. The latter stood on a dais in the centre of the room.

The others spilled in behind him and stared around. 'Wow,' said Rochelle, 'it's like something out of a sci-fi movie. All that's missing is the men in the white coats.'

'What on earth is a lab like this doing on an oil rig?' asked Linda.

'No mystery,' said Alex. 'They use it for analysing mineral samples, oil shale, mud and stuff like that.'

Paul shook his head. 'No. This is a *medical* lab. I recognise a lot of the gear. When I got out of college I spent a year working as a lab technician in a medical school. And it fits in with that air-lock thing out in the corridor. It's some kind of safety device to stop bacteria getting out . . .'

'Oh my God!' cried Chris 'you mean this place might be full of dangerous germs?'

Paul couldn't help smiling. She had a fetish against any kind of pollution and an accompanying mania about personal hygiene. 'Take it easy,' he said. 'No need to jump to any wild conclusions. The air-lock is probably just a precaution. Who knows, it may be there to stop contamination coming in from outside.'

'I hope you're right,' she said. 'I just wish we could find someone to talk to. Where *is* everyone? What happened to them?'

'Whatever happened they certainly left in a hurry,' said Linda. 'Look at this.' She pointed at a coffee cup sitting on one of the tables. 'It's half full.'

'Gee, just like the *Marie Celeste*,' said Rochelle, and gave a theatrical shudder. 'That ship where all the people disappeared right in the middle of their meal.'

'It was called the *Mary* Celeste, not Marie,' said Mark. 'And it wasn't such a big mystery as everyone thinks it was.'

'Oh yeah? How do *you* know?' demanded Rochelle.

'Yeah, pinhead,' said Alex belligerently. 'What the hell do you know about what really happened? You got psychic powers like your old lady too?'

They all looked expectantly at Mark, including Paul. Mark gave a resigned sigh. 'When I was a kid my father told me the story of the *Mary Celeste*. We were out alone on the yacht at the time, miles from anywhere. He wanted to scare me, I think, and he did a damned good job of it. Everytime I went out on the yacht with him after that – and he was always making me go on trips with him – I couldn't get the story out of my mind. Whenever we lost sight of land my imagination used to run riot. I expected to see God knows what come out of the water, or out of the sky, and grab us. So eventually, when I got older, I decided to do some checking up on the *Celeste* story . . .'

'How?' asked Paul.

Mark shrugged. 'Easy. The records are still on file with Lloyds of London. I arranged to go look at them. Turns out that the whole *Celeste* thing got wildly exaggerated by the newspapers at the time, and by writers since then. For example, the legend has it that all the lifeboats were on the ship when it was found but that isn't true. *One* of the boats was missing, which led the official enquiry to conclude that the ship encountered bad weather and the crew panicked and abandoned her in the mistaken belief she was sinking. There was certainly a lot of evidence that the ship had been through a storm . . .'

'So there goes another illusion,' said Paul with a grin. 'But it just goes to prove we shouldn't let ourselves get spooked by this place. We stay calm and loose until we figure out what the set-up is here.'

'Yes *sir*, Mr Boss-Man,' said Alex sarcastically. 'Whatever you say.' Then suddenly he bent down behind a chair and picked something up off the floor. Paul saw it was a white lab coat. And as Alex held it up a bra and a pair of white lace briefs fell out. Leering, Alex snatched up the briefs. 'Hey! They got women here.' To Paul's disgust he put them to his nose and made exaggerated sniffing noises. 'Mmm-mm, I'd sure like to meet the owner of these. You think they had some kind of orgy in here?'

'More likely she took them off because her clothes had become contaminated,' said Paul coldly.

Alex dropped the underwear as if it had burnt his fingers. He took a quick step backwards and stared at Paul with wide, scared eyes. 'Hey, what kind of shit are you pulling? *Contaminated?* How come?'

Paul couldn't resist twisting the knife. 'It's possible. There could have been a release of dangerous bacteria in here. Why else would someone strip off in the middle of a lab? Perhaps that's the reason this place seems deserted.'

'You don't really believe that, do you Paul?' asked Chris in a panicky voice.

Paul immediately regretted his words. For the sake of scoring a cheap shot against Alex he'd made things worse. He was supposed to be calming their fears, not scaring them even more. 'No, I guess not,' he told her reassuringly. 'If there was anything loose in the air I think this whole area would have been automatically sealed off. That airlock outside is probably designed to do just that.'

'Which still leaves us with the question of why the owner of these clothes took them all off,' said Linda. 'Look, her shoes are here too.'

'Perhaps there *was* an outbreak of something but it's all dissipated now,' suggested Mark.

'Yeah,' said Paul doubtfully. 'Even so maybe we should be careful about touching anything.' The latter was directed at Linda who was crouching down beside the clothes that Alex had dropped and examining them. 'Hey,' she said, 'There's an identification label on this coat. And a photograph too.'

Paul leaned over her shoulder and stared at the plastic covered badge she was pointing at. The small photo showed a very attractive blonde woman in her late 20s. He could just make out the name. 'Carol Soames,' he read aloud. '*Doctor* Carol Soames. I wonder where she is now.'

'*I* wonder if she's still alive,' said Chris darkly.

'Hey, has anyone but me noticed something weird about those clothes?' asked Rochelle.

'Like what?' asked Paul.

'The underwear was *inside* the coat.'

Paul frowned. 'Are you sure?'

'Yes, she's right,' said Linda. 'They fell *out* of the coat. Now why would anyone go to the trouble of doing that, especially if they were undressing in a hurry?'

'Who gives a shit?' muttered Alex, still casting anxious looks at his fingers as if expecting to see signs of contamination. 'I just hope I get to run into her before she has a chance to get dressed again.'

'God, you're so predictable, Alex,' said Chris with a grimace. 'There's more to life than sex, you know . . .'

'Yeah?' Alex's smile was ugly. 'How would you know? You've never slept with a real man.'

As he said this he turned and gave Mark a challenging stare but Mark just sighed and looked away.

'Okay,' said Paul quickly, 'Can we save the arguments for later? Right now we've got more important things to worry about.'

'Yes,' said Linda, 'Like where's the nearest bathroom. I'm bursting.'

'So am I,' said Rochelle. '*And* I'm starving.'

'Then let's get moving. We'll finish checking out this floor then go down to the next one. There's got to be *somebody* here.'

'And what if we don't find anyone?' asked Chris.

'Then we'll just make ourselves at home until someone turns up,' said Paul.

'Paul, what do you think this is?' Mark was standing next to the sculpture made of different coloured ping pong balls. It was at least eight feet high.

'It's obvious, jerk,' said Alex before Paul could reply. 'It's a model of a molecule. The balls are supposed to be atoms. We had one in our science room at high school.'

Paul shook his head. 'No, I don't think it is.'

'Then what is it, wise guy?'

'I think it's a model of a chromosome. See how the rows of ping pong balls spiral round each other. That's the famous "double helix". I think each represents a separate gene.'

There was silence in the room while they all stared at the model. Then Chris said, in a bleak voice, 'Genetic engineering.'

'What?' asked Mark.

'Genetic engineering. That's what they've been doing here. And I don't like it. I don't like it at all.'

Linda frowned. 'I don't get it. What would a genetic engineering lab be doing on an oil rig?'

'Exactly,' said Chris. 'What are they trying to hide?'

Three

As they continued along the corridor Linda pointed out something they hadn't noticed before. Suspended from the ceiling at regular intervals were more television cameras.

'Whatever they were doing here they certainly had tight security,' said Paul.

'Maybe they've still got it,' said Mark. 'Maybe there's someone at the end of those cameras. *I* feel like I'm being watched.'

'Then why don't they show themselves?' asked Linda.

'That's the 64,000 dollar question,' said Paul.

They checked the next room. It was another laboratory almost identical to the first. It was also empty. But, to their growing puzzlement, they did find more articles of discarded clothing. They were in three separate heaps – all male garments this time – and like before the underwear had been carefully placed *inside* the outer clothes. Even the socks were inside the shoes.

Paul felt baffled as he prodded through the clothes with a plastic ruler. 'This is crazy . . .' he muttered.

'Weirdos. We're dealing with weirdos here,' said Alex.

'It's creepy,' said Chris. She kept glancing nervously around, as if she expected something to jump out at them even though there was nowhere in the lab for anyone to hide.

Paul gave up his examination of the clothes. 'This is getting us nowhere. Let's move on.'

'Wouldn't it be better if we split up?' said Alex.

'No. I don't think it's a good idea.'

'What's the matter?' sneered Alex. 'Scared?'

Keeping control of his temper with an effort Paul said, 'No. I just think we should all stick together until we know what the situation is here.'

Alex suddenly reached inside his shirt. There was a *click* and Paul found himself looking at a six inch switch-blade being held directly under his nose. 'See, Mr Boss-Man, no need to worry. We run into anyone who tries to mess with us and I'll take care of them with this.'

Paul couldn't conceal his surprise. He had no idea that Alex was carrying the weapon. He'd never even seen it before. Would he have been so eager to pick arguments with Alex if he'd known, he wondered. One thing was certain – Alex was more than capable of using it on someone.

As calmly as he could he said, 'Very impressive, Alex, but put it away before you hurt yourself. I'm sure you're not going to need it.'

Alex's eyes went hard. 'You want to bet on that, *Boss*-Man?'

His meaning was obvious. It was a direct challenge but one that Paul had no choice but to ignore. Deliberately turning his back on Alex he headed for the door. 'Let's go,' he said casually.

But despite this display of bravado the muscles in his back tightened with fear. He knew he was going to feel like this from now on whenever Alex was behind him.

There were another six laboratories on the top floor, all of them deserted. Five were similar to the first two but one of them – the largest – was full of sophisticated computer equipment and other elaborate-looking electronic devices. 'There must be at least a hundred thousand pounds worth of gear in this lab alone,' said Paul in wonder.

'Yeah?' said Alex, looking around with new interest.

'Forget it, Alex. You wouldn't be able to carry it very far anyway.'

Apart from the labs there were also a number of store rooms containing various scientific and medical supplies, and also a miniature power station housing two compact, diesel-powered generators. It, too, was deserted.

Finally they came to a communications room and it was here they received the first of a series of nasty surprises.

It had been completely wrecked. The expensive-looking transmitters had been smashed to pieces and the floor was littered with broken equipment. It was as if a bomb had gone off.

'I guess we won't be making any phone calls home,' said Paul, surveying the grim scene.

'Someone sure got pissed off in here,' said Alex. 'I wonder why.'

'Hey, look at this!' Rochelle was bending down and pulling something out from under a pile of debris. It was an automatic rifle.

Alex immediately rushed over and snatched it out of her hands. 'Wow, it's an M16!' he cried excitedly. He began to examine its mechanism with practised hands, treating it like an old friend. But then it probably was, Paul realised. He remembered that Alex had spent some time in the US Army before being dishonourably discharged for dealing in drugs.

'Is it in working order?' Paul asked him, trying to hide his alarm.

'Sure is.' Alex pulled out the magazine. 'And loaded too.'

'It looks pretty light,' said Paul, keeping his tone relaxed.

'The stock and grip are made of hollow fibre glass. It don't weigh much more than a .22,' said Alex, pleased to show off his knowledge. 'But it packs a hell of a bigger punch than a .22. It takes 5.63 ammo and you can fire it like an ordinary rifle, one round at a time, or you can put the selector on "Auto" like this . . .' He demonstrated the selector on the side of the weapon, '. . . And fire off eighteen rounds in the blink of an eye. But that's not wise 'cause the magazine only holds eighteen rounds. Best just to touch the trigger when it's on "auto", that way you get off a burst of about three bullets . . .' He cocked the gun and then said, 'Right, now it's got one up the spout and is all ready and rarin' to go.'

'Fine,' said Paul calmly. He held out his hand. 'Now hand it over.'

Alex's eyebrows shot upwards in surprise. 'Are you kidding?'

'No. I want that gun.'

Alex's mouth took on an ugly line. 'Tough shit.' He swung the barrel around until it was pointing at Paul's stomach. The atmosphere in the room became electric.

Then Mark cried, 'Hey, I've found another one!'

Paul turned to see Mark pulling a second M16 from under an overturned chair. He reached out for it. Mark was about to hand it over to him when Alex rasped, 'Don't give it to him!'

Mark froze.

'Ignore him,' said Paul with the same calm voice. 'Give me the gun, Mark.' Inside he was a turmoil of nerves. His body tensed, waiting for the crash of Alex's M16 and the mule-kick of the bullet. Mark slowly extended the gun to him. Paul took hold of it.

There was no gun shot.

Paul checked to see if his weapon was loaded, studiously ignoring Alex. When he saw it was loaded he looked at Alex and smiled at him. 'Well?'

With a scowl Alex lowered his M16. Paul felt a great wave of relief wash over him. A crisis had been averted – for the time being.

Chris gave a nervous laugh, 'Oh good. Now both the big men have a toy each and we can all relax.'

'Shut your dumb mouth, you stupid cow,' snarled Alex.

'Oh, for God's sake, why can't we stop all this fighting among ourselves and concentrate on finding out what *happened* here,' said Linda angrily. 'For a start I'd like to know what weapons like those are doing on an oil rig.'

'Well, we already know it's no ordinary oil rig,' said Paul, thankful for Linda's contribution.

'Hey, you guys. More clothes!' It was Rochelle, holding up what appeared to be the jacket of some sort of uniform. It was dark blue but covered with several rust-like stains.

They gathered round her for a closer look. On the lapel was a badge that read 'Security' together with a small photograph of an earnest young man with a crew-cut.

'Must have belonged to the owner of one of the guns,' said Paul. Then he noticed something else. So did the others.

'Jesus,' whispered Chris. 'It's been *slashed* by something. A knife.'

'Or claws,' said Mark. 'The cuts are parallel, see . . .'

It was then that Paul realised what the stains were.

Dried blood.

On the second level, to Linda's intense relief, they found toilets. But that was the only discovery they made that gave them any comfort. Level Two, as it was officially called according to various signs on the walls, was much the same as the top one. Gleaming white corridors linked a complex of laboratories and store rooms – and all devoid of human life.

More bundles of clothes were found, several of them ripped and blood-stained like the ones in the communications room but the majority were unmarked. And all, inexplicably, had the underwear inside the outer garments. There were also signs that outbreaks of violence had occurred. There were bullet holes in a few of the walls, some broken doors and one of the store rooms had been burnt out.

By the time they reached the second level from the bottom they were all feeling thoroughly exhausted and were no longer bothering to do more than just look briefly into each room they passed. They were all empty, of course, and no one answered their increasingly weary cries of 'Hallo! Anyone here?'

This level was the same as the ones above except for two things. One was a long, narrow room full of empty cages of varying sizes. And despite the smell of disinfectant in the air it had a pronounced zoo-like odour.

'Phew,' said Rochelle, wrinkling her nose. 'What the hell did they keep in here? It smells like Alex's socks.'

Paul began to read out the labels on the empty cages. 'Rhesus monkeys, Chimpanzees, Marmosets, Orangoutangs . . .' He moved on down the row of cages. '. . . And here there were domestic cats, guinea pigs, dogs, rats – *lots* of rats. These must have been used for experiments.'

'Bastards,' said Chris who was, of course, a strong anti-vivisectionist.

'But where *are* they all?' wondered Linda aloud.

'They must have been evacuated along with the people when whatever went wrong here went wrong,' said Mark.

'That doesn't make sense. If that was the case the cages wouldn't be here either,' said Paul.

'And have you noticed something even odder?' asked Chris. 'All of them are still locked. Why on earth would anyone go to the bother of locking the cages after the animals had been removed?'

No one had an answer.

At the end of the room were a pair of swing doors that opened into an aquarium area. Illuminated with the same eerie kind of violet light that had been in the airlock it contained rows of glass tanks of different sizes. And like the cages these, too, were all empty.

'Curiouser and curiouser . . .' whispered Linda.

There was a strange atmosphere in the aquarium, exaggerated no doubt by the lighting and also the sounds made by all the bubbling oxygen appliances in the tanks. But it was the *emptiness* of the place that was so unsettling . . .

'Don't tell me,' muttered Rochelle. 'They evacuated all the fish too.'

'I don't like it here. Let's leave, *now*,' said Chris.

'More bad vibes?' answered Alex.

'They must have had some really big fish in here,' said Mark. 'Look at the size of *that* tank.' He was pointing at one that was at least twenty feet long. Paul went and read the label on the front of it. 'Just says "Carcharodon". Anyone know what that means?'

'Nope,' said Linda and shivered. 'I agree with Chris, let's get out of here. It gives me the creeps too.'

The other intriguing feature on this level was a room packed with TV equipment. It was obviously the control point for all the cameras they had spotted throughout the platform. There were eight monitor screens positioned around a large console and all of them were functioning, each one showing a different part of the rig.

'It's as if someone had walked out of here a moment before we arrived,' said Chris.

'They probably did,' said Alex. 'And I'll bet you this is from where our shy host operated the crane that picked us up.'

'It's possible,' said Paul doubtfully, staring at the equipment.

'I wish they'd stop hiding from us,' said Linda. 'It's crazy. Why are they acting this way?'

'As we said earlier. They must have something to hide,' said Mark.

'Then why haven't they prevented us from wandering around?' she asked.

Mark shook his head. 'Don't ask me.'

Paul, meanwhile, had made another discovery. Racks and racks of video cassettes, all of them carefully labelled with some kind of code. He picked one of them up and examined it. 'Wonder what's on this, if anything.'

'We should run it through and see,' said Linda. 'There must be a video playback machine somewhere in all this stuff. It might give us a clue as to what was going on here.'

'It would take *days* to run through all those cassettes,' protested Rochelle. 'Look at it later. Right now let's try and find where they keep the food and the beds in this place. I'm about ready to drop.'

The others agreed with her so they then headed down to the fifth and final level. Level One, it turned out, was entirely devoted to living space and consisted of sleeping quarters, kitchens and recreational rooms. Paul estimated that it would have housed at least 250 people . . .

They made a cursory examination of the place and found, as they now expected, it was devoid of human life. Or at least it *appeared* to be – they couldn't be sure because several of the doors were locked but there was no response when they banged on the doors. Deciding to check them out later they retired to one of the kitchens to have something to eat.

The kitchen they chose turned out to be well-stocked with both frozen and tinned foods, revealing, if nothing else, that the original inhabitants of the rig ate well. On Paul's advice they used only the tinned food, making a quick stew out of a variety of ingredients. Similarly they ignored the water from the taps and drank only mineral water from sealed bottles and tinned fruit juice.

The meal made them all feel much better. Even Mark's appearance improved, to Paul's relief, as he'd been worried that Mark might have been coming down with something serious. Even better, the food had the effect of mellowing Alex a little. By the end of the meal his habitual mood of glowering antagonism seemed thankfully absent though Paul was sure this would only be a temporary change.

It was past ten p.m. when they finished eating and the women were all anxious to find somewhere to sleep as soon as possible but Paul insisted they check out the locked rooms before they turned in.

It took another hour before they had broken down all the locked doors and investigated all the rooms. They didn't find anyone but what they did find didn't improve their state of minds. In all the locked rooms there were more piles of empty clothing – but in every case the doors had been locked from the *inside*.

What they found in one of the recreational rooms was particularly disturbing – a large mound of clothing piled up against the far wall. Paul estimated that there was enough to clothe twelve people. They also found another two M16s and a revolver – which brought the total of guns they'd so far collected to eighteen – and what appeared to be two make-shift flame-throwers.

'They *must* have had an orgy in here,' said Alex and gave a

dirty snigger, but Paul was aware of his underlying nervousness. And he had to admit he was feeling increasingly uneasy
himself. Something *weird* had happened on the oil rig and until
he found out exactly what he wouldn't be able to shake off the
fear that it could happen again. To them.

'It's as if a group of people were all backed against the wall,
facing the door, and then simply vanished out of their clothes,'
said Mark softly.

'Hey, don't say that,' said Rochelle angrily, 'you're scaring
me.'

'I can't understand how they got out with the door locked
from the inside,' said Linda.

'Perhaps they *did* get dissolved,' said Chris nervously, 'by
some kind of new biological weapon. A gas or airborne virus
that eats human flesh . . .'

'Uh-oh, she's dropped her bag of cookies again,' muttered
Alex.

'What are you talking about, Chris?' asked Paul.

'I think this place is a secret government germ warfare establishment. It ties in with those big models of chromosomes we
kept finding in the labs. They were creating illegal biological
weapons with genetic engineering. And one of them got out
of control . . .'

'But this is an American-owned rig,' said Linda.

Chris shrugged, 'So the American government are behind
it. It would be typical of them to set up a dangerous weapons
establishment right on another country's doorstep.'

'Hey, hold it,' protested Alex, 'that's my crowd you're slan-
dering there. The greatest country in the world.'

'Any country that can produce both Charles Manson *and*
you, Alex, I have sincere doubts about,' said Linda sweetly.

Alex scowled at her. 'One of these days I'm going to take
that smart mouth of yours, Linda, and make it look like your
ass-hole's twin sister.'

'Okay, cool it,' warned Paul. Then, 'Actually Chris might
be half-right. This place could be some sort of clandestine

genetic engineering establishment. One thing's for certain – is hasn't been used for oil drilling for a long time, if it ever was at all. Right where we're standing now should be full of drilling and pumping equipment, storage tanks and other stuff. This platform is just a shell, a clever piece of camouflage for all the labs . . .'

'Which means,' said Linda, 'that whatever they do in here is definitely illegal.'

'Yes,' agreed Paul, 'and that's probably why whoever it is who's been left to look after this place is staying out of our way. They don't want to answer any embarrassing questions.'

'Fine. That's settled then,' said Rochelle, yawning, 'now let's go get some sleep.'

'Good idea,' said Paul, 'we can resume the search in the morning.'

'I don't like to think there's someone prowling around while we sleep,' said Chris.

Alex hefted his M16 in a menacing fashion. 'Nothing to worry about on that score. Nobody's gonna mess with us. We got guns and plenty of ammunition.'

Chris pointed at the piles of empty clothing. 'So had they.'

Four

They chose three cabins near to the kitchen where they'd eaten. The cabins each had four bunks but all three couples wanted to be on their own. It was the first opportunity for anything approaching privacy since they'd left Morocco. On the yacht they'd been obliged to share the vessel's one large cabin and, of course, since the sinking the situation had been much worse.

As a result the foremost thing on Alex's mind as he closed the door of his cabin was getting laid. It had been nearly two weeks since he and Rochelle had made love and for him that was a record he intended he would never beat.

He locked the door then turned and wrapped his muscular arms around her, squeezing so hard she grunted with pain.

'Okay Ro,' he said, 'we got a lot of catching up to do, so let's get goin' . . .' He ground his pelvis hard against hers then started to push her backwards towards the nearest bunk. He stopped when she suddenly brought her right knee up sharply into his groin.

'*Cunt* . . .' he hissed as he let go of her and doubled up, his face white from the pain.

She regarded him calmly. She was never frightened of him, no matter how aggressive he became. She was confident she could always handle him. 'I'm tired, Alex. *Very* tired. I'm going to sleep right now.' She began to undo her shirt. 'You're going to have to wait until morning.'

'I should break your jaw,' he gasped.

'Yeah? You just try, mate. I'd make you regret it for the rest of your life. So just shut up and go to bed like a good boy.'

He quickly forgot his pain as he watched her take off her shirt and then unzip her jeans. His eyes took in her tight, round breasts and the provocative curve of her muscular buttocks – the latter a legacy of her ice-skating days – as she bent down to slip out of her jeans. His anger began to fade too as his desire increased. Of all the women he'd ever known Rochelle had a body that came the closest to his sexual ideal. She had him where it counted the most, he realised ruefully – by the balls.

'Hey, Ro . . . I was only kidding.' His voice took on an unpleasant, pleading whine. 'You know that.'

'Yeah, sure.' She was naked now and as she climbed onto the bunk and got under the single blanket he received a glimpse of her pink, shaved crotch which excited him even more. He could feel himself getting harder as he thought of the last time he had shaved her – it was something he insisted upon doing to all his women. It had been in the dingy hotel room in Morocco – it had been around lunch time on a blazing hot day and they had both been as high as hell on hashish. Ro had lain there on the big bed in the bright sunshine while he had worked on her as slowly as possible, taking elaborate pains with every stroke of the cut-throat razor. Afterwards they had had some of the best sex he could remember . . .

He swallowed dryly as he got to his feet and went over to her bunk. 'Hey, c'mon Ro. Don't be a bitch. I'm feeling really horny.'

She looked up at him through bleary, red-rimmed eyes and said drowsily, 'I'm not kidding, Alex. I'm dead tired. I've *got* to get some sleep. In the morning I'll do anything you goddamn want but you're just going to have to wait.' Then she turned over on her side, with her back to him. 'Put the light out, will you?'

Cursing under his breath he went and switched out the light then stretched out on the other bottom bunk, not bothering to get undressed. He felt really tempted to go and screw her brains out whether she wanted it or not but he knew it wouldn't be worth the consequences. He needed her too much to risk wrecking their relationship completely.

He had been lying there in the dark for about fifteen minutes when he heard a soft tapping at the door. Warily he got up, put the light on and called, 'Who's there?'

'It's me, Chris. I've got to talk to you, Alex.'

As he opened the door Rochelle moaned and turned over. 'What's going on?' she asked sleepily.

'I'm sorry to disturb you guys,' Chris apologised in a loud whisper, 'But it's Mark. He's in a bad way and only Alex can help.'

Rochelle frowned. '*Alex* can help Mark? I must be dreaming.'

Chris turned to Alex who had now closed the door and was leaning against it with an amused, self-satisfied expression. 'You know what I'm talking about,' she told him.

'Do I?' he asked blandly.

'Mark's going cold turkey and he's in a bad way. He thinks you've still got some junk with you. He lost all his when the boat went down.'

Rochelle propped herself up on one elbow, looking more

alert now. 'Chris, what the hell are you going on about?'

Turning to her, Chris said, 'Mark's a heroin addict. Has been for the last six months, thanks to Alex here. Surely you've noticed the way he looks these days, and the way he's been behaving since we've been adrift?'

'Yeah, but I just thought that was shock . . .'

'The reason for the Morocco trip wasn't just to buy grass,' continued Chris grimly. 'Alex had talked Mark into doing a heroin deal as well, with Mark putting up most of the capital, of course. Paul and Linda didn't know anything about it. Alex knew they wouldn't want anything to do with smuggling hard drugs. But I thought *you* would have been let in on it by now.'

'Is this true?' Rochelle asked Alex.

He gave a casual shrug of his large shoulders. 'Yeah. I didn't tell you because you can't keep your damn trap shut about anything for more than ten seconds. But I was gonna give you a cut of the profits, Ro, I swear . . .'

She grimaced. 'Yeah, I'll bet. But I would have appreciated being told we were doing a heroin run as well as just grass. Do you realise what would have happened if we'd have been caught? We all knew the risks we were taking with the grass but . . .'

'*Have* you got any left?' Chris interrupted impatiently. 'If Mark doesn't get a fix soon I don't know what's going to happen to him. I'm afraid he might even die . . . he's never been very fit. I don't think he has the constitution to stand going completely cold turkey without any medical help . . .' Her eyes began to fill with tears and her voice broke.

Alex held up a hand. 'Take it easy, Chris. Yeah, I still got my stash . . . see . . .' He undid his pants belt and pulled out his shirt. Round his lower waist was a flat belt consisting of a series of small plastic pouches. 'About £100,000's worth here, nice and dry. I took the precaution of getting this waterproof money belt.'

Chris stared at the belt and gave a sigh of relief. 'Will you let him have some? He said he'll pay you later . . .'

Alex gave another shrug. 'Sure. Anything to help a buddy. You got a needle?'

'What?' Chris blinked at him in surprise. She hadn't expected it to be so easy. It was totally unlike Alex to do a favour for anyone without being coerced into it, especially if it involved money. 'Oh, yes, Mark picked up a couple of hypodermics from one of the labs this afternoon.' She paused, then said, 'Thanks Alex. I really appreciate this.'

'Hey, don't act so surprised,' he said, 'you know you can always rely on ol' Alex when the chips are down. Now come on, let's go fix up Mark.' He opened the door for her and, after nodding goodnight to Rochelle, Chris hurried out.

'You go back to sleep, honey,' Alex told Rochelle, 'I'll try not to wake you when I come back.' He turned out the light and shut the door before she could say anything. In the darkness she lay back on the bunk. Her suspicions had been aroused by Alex's uncharacteristic readiness to help someone out but right now she was too tired to give a damn. And within seconds she began to slide down into sleep . . .

To Chris's surprise Alex pulled her hand away before she could open the door to her and Mark's cabin and silently indicated that she should follow him. Puzzled, she followed him along the corridor and into an empty cabin about four doors along from where the others were.

'What's the matter?' she asked as he closed the door and turned to face her with a smug grin. 'Why are we in here?'

He didn't say anything but just looked her up and down slowly. It was as if he was staring right through her clothes. With a sick feeling she realised what was on his mind.

'Take your shirt off,' he said suddenly. His voice sounded harsh.

She only hesitated for a short time but came quickly to the conclusion that there was no way out of this if she expected to get the heroin for Mark. She'd been stupid to think Alex would give it free of charge . . .

'Nice tits,' said Alex after she had taken off the shirt. 'Not great but they'll do.' His smile got uglier. 'Now everything else.'

When she was standing completely naked before him he said. 'You any good at giving head?'

'No,' she said quickly.

'Well, you will be after this,' he said, and laughed.

'Alex, please . . .'

'Better hurry up before I change my mind about helping Mark out.'

She almost gave in to panic at that point but steeled herself and knelt down in front of him. Matter-of-factly she unzipped his fly and tugged his hard penis out of his pants. He was bigger than Mark, she saw, and she tried not to gag as she took it into her mouth. She was vaguely shocked to find he tasted like Mark. And then followed one of the worst experiences of her life as she sucked and tongued his erection for what seemed an eternity. The whole time he gave her a series of running instructions, telling her when to go fast, slow and when to caress or squeeze his scrotum with her fingertips. Finally, to her relief, she sensed that he was getting near to coming. He began to thrust deep into the back of her throat, practically choking her each time, but she didn't care – so eager was she to get it over with . . .

She screwed her eyes shut and dug her nails into her hand to take away the sensation of him spurting into her mouth. She thought he was never going to stop but eventually he did and slowly withdrew. She opened her eyes, swallowed heavily then wiped her lips with the back of her hand. Shakily she got to her feet and faced him. 'Okay, you sonofabitch, now you go and take care of Mark.'

He looked back at her with hooded eyes. There seemed to be a kind of film over them. Then, with a thick voice he said, 'Not so fast. We're not finished yet.' He reached out and squeezed her left breast roughly. 'That was just for starters. Get back on your knees and take it slower this time. When you've got me hard again I'll show you a new kind of game I'll bet you and that wimp have never thought of playing . . .'

Somehow she managed not to scream.

Paul and Linda moved together on their single bed, their slow sinuous love the focus of their being. Their bodies slid slickly on each other and their hands gently touched the flesh both knew so well. Paul was relaxed for the first time in days – he had no thoughts, only emotions. But then Linda suddenly stopped. 'Listen, do you hear that?' she whispered urgently.

'Oh no, not again,' he moaned. Earlier they had been distracted by the sound of the others moving up and down the corridor, opening and shutting doors. He had no idea what they were up to but he couldn't care less.

'It sounds like something big being dragged along the passageway,' said Linda. 'Some kind of sack . . .'

Paul sighed and cocked his head to listen. She was right. It *did* sound as if a heavy sack was being dragged along outside.

The noise stopped at their door and then, after a brief pause, it was replaced by a curious scratching sound, as if a small animal was pawing at the door.

'What *is* that?' asked Linda in a frightened whisper.

'Probably Alex trying to be funny,' said Paul. He rolled off her and got up as quietly as possible. As he approached the door he felt a prickle of unease travel up the bare skin along his spine. It occurred to him it might not be Alex after all but one of the missing laboratory animals.

'Don't open the door!' cried Linda in a low, urgent voice.

'Don't worry, I'm not going to,' he assured her as he warily pressed his ear against the wood.

At that precise moment there came a tremendous crash and he recoiled in shock as the whole door shuddered under some enormous impact from the other side.

Simultaneously there was a bellowing roar that sounded totally unlike anything Paul had ever heard before.

Then the door began to splinter inwards . . .

Five

Though partially stunned Paul reacted with speed. He made a dive for the M16 lying on the floor beside the bunk, snatched it up then spun round and aimed it at the door. There were now five long fissures in the top half of the door and even as he looked more began to appear. The terrible bellowing sound continued, almost drowning out Linda's high-pitched scream.

He pulled the trigger. The weapon's selector had obviously been left on 'Auto' as the entire magazine emptied itself within seconds. The bullets passed through the door as if it wasn't there and from the other side the angry bellowing immediately became a shriek of pain . . .

The door stopped shuddering and there was the sound of something very big and heavy rebounding off the opposite wall of the passageway. Then the shrieking began to fade as the animal, or whatever it was, began to move off down the corridor.

They followed its progress to the end of the corridor then heard it begin to go up the stairs leading to the level above. There were a few more distant crashes then silence.

Paul looked at Linda. She had retreated to the far end of the bunk and was pressed back into a corner, her knees drawn up in front of her. Her face was completely white. He had never seen anyone look so frightened before and suspected his own face presented a similar picture.

'Paul . . .' she said weakly.

He swallowed and tried to give her a reassuring grin. He didn't succeed. 'It's okay, it's gone now . . .'

He put the now useless M16 down and began to struggle into his pants. 'Get dressed,' he told her. 'We've got to check on the others then try and track down whatever animal that was and finish it off.'

'Finish . . . it . . . off,' she repeated blankly. 'Paul . . . what *was* it?'

'I don't know, a bear maybe. Here . . .' He tossed her clothes at her then picked up the loaded .38 revolver they'd brought into the cabin along with the M16. He went back to the shattered door and listened intently for a few moments then slowly opened it. The .38 felt ridiculously small and puny in his hand and he knew instinctively it would be useless against whatever it was that had tried to break in.

But there was nothing outside.

Giving a deep sigh of relief he stepped out into the passageway and called, 'Hey, everybody! The coast is clear! Are you people okay?'

One of the doors opened and Rochelle emerged. She was stark naked and carrying Alex's M16. She looked dazed and her face was completely drained of colour.

Mark emerged next, also alone; pale, shaking and covered in sweat. He looked as if he was about to collapse. Then, to Paul's surprise, Alex and Chris came out of the same cabin a number of doors away. Chris was hastily doing up her shirt and her face looked red and puffy, as if she'd been crying. But, as if by unspoken agreement, this unexpected development was obviously going to be ignored – at least for the time being. Right now there were more important things on everyone's mind . . .

'Jesus,' breathed Rochelle, 'what happened? What was making all that *noise*? I've never heard anything like it . . .'

Paul shook his head. 'I don't know. It must have been some kind of animal. None of you saw anything?'

'You kidding?' said Alex, taking the gun away from Rochelle. She seemed reluctant to let go of it. 'No way I was gonna take a look-see outside with the sound that thing was making. Sounded like a bull elephant on heat . . .'

'Paul, look at the door.' It was Linda. She was pointing at their cabin door. The wood was scored with deep parallel grooves as if made by giant claws.

'Who did all the shooting? You?' Alex asked Paul.

'Yes. I emptied the gun through the door,' said Paul. 'Must have hit it a couple of times at least. Sure sounded in pain afterwards.'

'You hit it more than a couple of times,' said Alex confidently. He was examining the wall on the other side of the passageway. 'See. Only five holes. Means you put thirteen bullets into it.'

Paul stared at the five bullet holes. They were like craters. He felt a chill run through him. *Thirteen* similar holes would be in the creature he'd shot – yet it had been able to walk away. Just what the hell *was* it?

He jumped as a loud *thump* sound came from above. Then there was the distant sound of breaking glass and another muffled crash.

They all stared at the ceiling.

'It's on the next level. Right above us,' whispered Chris.

Paul's first instinct was to run into the nearest cabin and barricade the door but he forced himself to say, with as much calmness as he could muster, 'Okay, Alex and I are going after it. Someone get me another M16. Mark, you and the girls lock yourself in one of the cabins and don't come out until we give you the all-clear.'

Alex looked at him in alarm. 'Hey, what's all this *we* stuff? If you want to play Great White Hunter go ahead. My ass is staying down here. The thing's probably dying anyway – nothing can stand up to an M16 at that range. Let's just wait until it croaks . . .'

'If you're going up there *I'm* coming with you,' Linda told Paul firmly.

'Me too,' said Rochelle. 'I can fire a gun just as well as you can, Paul. And probably better than *he* can.' She jerked her thumb at Alex.

There was another loud crash from overhead.

'Well, whoever's coming, follow me,' said Paul grimly. 'I want to get to the bottom of this, one way or the other. Whatever that thing is up there it's the answer to the whole screwy business.'

In the end they all went. With Paul in the lead they quietly and warily climbed the stairs to the next level. In the distance they could still hear the periodic explosions of sound. Thirteen bullets or not the creature didn't seem to be getting any weaker. And there was the problem of the blood . . .

It was Rochelle who drew their attention to this as they were going up the stairs. 'Hey, I've just noticed another weird thing,' she said. 'There isn't any blood. There's none here and there wasn't any on the floor in the passageway.'

'Yeah, Ro's right,' said Alex, who was bringing up the rear.

'Perhaps Paul didn't shoot it after all,' said Chris nervously. 'He might have missed completely.'

'Please don't say that,' said Linda and shuddered.

'If I missed where are those thirteen bullets?' asked Paul.

At the top of the stairs they paused. The sounds had stopped. Ahead of them another of the pristine, brightly-lit corridors stretched into the distance. There was no sign of any animal, large or small. There was no sign of anything.

They all jumped as something heavy, like a filing cabinet, crashed to the floor. The sound appeared to come from a room about twenty yards down the corridor.

Paul checked to see that the safety catch was off on the M16. He noticed that the palms of his hands were slippery with nervous sweat. He gripped the weapon tighter. 'Let's go,' he whispered.

As they approached the door Paul kept expecting it to burst open and God knows what to fly out straight for him. He thought of the claw marks in the bedroom door . . .

But it stayed shut. Silently he indicated to Alex that he take up position on the other side. Reluctantly Alex obeyed. His face was white with strain. Paul had never seen him like this before.

Then, when the others were in position too, guns at the ready, Paul took a deep breath and reached out for the door handle. Deep down he was praying that it would be locked. He didn't want to admit it but he would have given anything not to have to open that door . . .

His prayers were answered but not in the way he expected.

Just as his fingers were about to touch the round, polished handle the door suddenly opened.

Paul almost pulled the trigger on the M16 but stopped himself just in time. He stared with amazement at the figure in the doorway and then almost burst out laughing with relief.

The man was small, plump and balding. With his white coat and glasses he looked like the scientist in *The Muppet Show*. He stared at them all with an expression of mild surprise, as if coming unexpectedly face-to-face with six armed strangers was an everyday experience for him. 'Oh, hello,' he said, in a thin, high-pitched voice, 'I was just on my way to see you. Sorry I wasn't able to meet you earlier – I was unavoidably detained . . .' He gave a brief smile.

Paul was trying to peer past him into the room. It was a lab of some kind. It was littered with smashed equipment but it seemed empty. Where was the animal?

'Who the hell are you?' Paul asked brusquely. 'And where's the thing that was making all that noise?'

'My name?' He frowned, then his face brightened, 'I'm Dr Shelley. Dr Gordon Shelley.' He sounded pleased to have remembered his own name. 'And as for the *thing*, I suppose you're referring to Charlie. But don't worry, we've got him under control again. He won't bother you any more tonight, that I promise you.'

'Who the fuck is Charlie?' growled Alex, rising from his crouch beside the door.

'Who is Charlie?' said Shelley. 'Ah, that's a little difficult to explain right now. Why don't you return to your rooms and get some sleep. I'll talk to you in the morning. Yes. The morning . . .' He frowned again. 'Tell me, what *day* is it today?'

'Uh, Wednesday, I think,' said Paul. He looked at Linda for confirmation. She nodded.

'And the month?' asked Shelley anxiously.

'June, of course,' said Paul.

'*Still* June?' Shelley looked surprised. 'It seems so much

longer since ... since ...' His voice trailed away and his face went blank. Then he suddenly smiled at them and said, 'Please forgive me. I'm not myself these days. Oh, not myself indeed!' He started to laugh. 'Ah, amazing that one can still retain a sense of humour in spite of everything – at least I *think* it's my sense of humour ...' He stopped smiling and blinked at them in surprise as if he was just seeing them for the first time. 'We've got to get you off the rig. Yes, as soon as possible. For your own sakes.'

Alex took a step forward and grabbed Shelley by the front of his coat. 'Listen, professor, cut the bullshit and tell me what's goin' on here! And where is that goddamn animal that made such a racket earlier?'

Calmly, Shelley reached up, took hold of Alex's wrist and pushed his hand away. He did it without any visible effort and Paul noted the look of surprise on Alex's face.

'The animal is where it can't disturb you again, I assure you. Now please return to your rooms. I'll explain everything tomorrow. Goodnight.'

Before they could react he ducked back into the lab and closed the door. They heard the click of a lock and then silence. Angrily, Alex began to bang on the door. 'Hey, professor! We're not finished with you yet! Open this goddamn door!'

But there was no response from inside and finally he gave up. 'Now what do we do?' he growled at Paul.

Paul shrugged. 'Do what he said, I guess.'

'But how can we be sure that animal won't come back?' asked Chris.

'We're just going to have to take his word for it. Nothing else we can do until morning. But we stay on our guard.'

'Well, I don't trust that mother,' said Alex. 'He sounded crazy to me. Completely off his rocker. I mean, what kind of scientist doesn't even know what friggin' month it is?'

'There was something very *weird* about him,' said Chris in a hushed voice. 'Didn't you all feel it? The vibrations he was giving off – I've never experienced anything like it before.'

'Screw your vibrations,' sneered Alex, 'I'll tell you one thing about the little creep, he's *strong* . . .' Alex rubbed his wrist. 'He almost broke my goddamn arm.'

The next morning Dr Shelley had disappeared. The door to the lab was open but there was no sign of him. They wandered around for awhile calling his name then went back to the level below and had a breakfast of baked beans and coffee in the kitchen they'd used the night before.

No one had slept much during the night and they all looked pretty tired though Paul was relieved to see that Mark seemed to have made a recovery. His face had lost its unhealthy pallor and he no longer appeared feverish.

'So who's got any bright ideas?' asked Rochelle as she spooned the last of her large helping of beans into her mouth. She had the biggest appetite of them all but never put on any weight.

'We go and have another look for Dr Shelley,' said Paul.

'I don't trust him,' said Alex sullenly. 'He's up to something.'

'Well, he was right about the animal – this "Charlie" thing,' said Linda. 'It didn't come back again last night.'

'I'd still give anything to know what it is,' said Paul. 'It must be one of their lab animals but what *kind*? The sound it made – I never heard any animal make a sound like that before, and we used to live near a zoo when I was a kid.'

'Perhaps it's a *new* kind of animal,' said Chris.

They all looked at her. 'What do you mean?' asked Linda.

'This place is a secret laboratory, right? Well I think they were carrying out illegal genetic experiments here. And that thing that tried to break into your cabin last night was one of them.'

'You mean it could be a mutated rat or a giant guinea pig? Hey, come on Chris, that's crazy. You've been reading too much science fiction,' said Mark.

Paul said carefully, 'I think Chris might have something. I think they *were* doing genetic engineering experiments here

– ones they didn't want anyone to know about. And whatever they made here got out of control.'

'But *what?*' asked Mark. 'What were they trying to make?'

'Only Dr Shelley can answer that.'

'I think we should get away from this place right now,' said Linda. 'Let's not bother looking for Dr Shelley any more. Let's just get the hell out of here.' There was an edge of desperation in her voice that Paul found disturbing. He reached over and patted her hand.

Alex sniggered at her. 'And just how are we gonna do that? It's a long swim to Scotland from here.'

Linda gave him a cold look. 'There are lifeboats. Several of them. I saw them when we first arrived.'

'But we'd be right back where we started,' pointed out Rochelle. 'I don't fancy being adrift in a little boat again. At least here we're warm and dry and have got lots of food and drink. *And* toilets.'

'Their boats are much bigger than ours was. They're enclosed and they've probably got motors too. And we can take plenty of supplies with us.' She turned to Paul. 'What do you think?'

'It's worth considering,' he said thoughtfully. 'If we can't find Shelley by late afternoon perhaps we should just get in one of the boats and get out of here. I don't like the idea of spending another night on the platform. "Charlie" might get restless again.'

'Do you know *how* to launch a lifeboat?' asked Chris doubtfully.

'No,' he admitted. 'In fact I think I'll go check one of them out right now. It's just occurred to me they might contain emergency radio beacons. It's possible we could send out a distress signal. Anyone want to come with me?' He got to his feet.

'I will,' said Mark, rising too. 'I could do with some fresh air.'

'Yeah, you two hot-shots go have fun,' said Alex. 'I'll stay here and guard the women.'

'Huh. And who's going to guard us from *you?*' asked Linda, only half-jokingly.

Alex contrived to look pained. 'I'm a very misunderstood person. It's the story of my life.'

'You'd better watch out your life story doesn't come to an abrupt end,' said Chris coldly.

He gave her an unpleasant leer. 'Tough talk, baby. You shouldn't speak that way to the guy who does you such big favours. You *owe* me, kid, and don't forget it.'

'I owe *you?* Like hell I do.' Her face began to redden with anger. 'You got paid a hundred times over, you bastard . . .'

'Hey, let's get on with it,' said Mark hurriedly and headed towards the door. Puzzled, Paul followed him. Once outside in the corridor he asked Mark what it had all been about. Mark said he had no idea. Paul knew he was lying but didn't pursue the matter. He presumed it had something to do with Chris and Alex coming out of the same room together last night. Whatever was going on meant trouble ahead, simply because it involved Alex, but he didn't have the time to be worried abut it now.

When they emerged onto the catwalk they were surprised to see that the weather had deteriorated badly since their arrival the day before. There was now a strong wind blowing and a sizeable swell. They both stared worriedly at the grey, heaving sea. 'I'm not sure I fancy going boating in *that* sea,' said Mark finally.

'Me neither,' said Paul. 'But maybe conditions will have improved by tonight.'

But when they reached the first of the lifeboats they realised it wouldn't matter if the weather improved or not. The hull of the boat had been smashed in.

There were five other large lifeboats suspended from various sections of the platform and, as Paul and Mark suspected, they too had been similarly sabotaged.

'We're trapped here,' said Mark as they surveyed the sixth and final boat. It had several gaping holes in its side. 'Aren't we?'

Paul picked up the remains of the shattered radio beacon. It had been the same with the other boats – all the beacons had been destroyed. He sighed. 'We're trapped all right. Someone on this rig enjoys our company so much they don't want us to leave.' He threw the pieces of the transmitter back into the boat. 'But we're going to beat them. Somehow.'

Mark shook his head. 'I don't think so,' he said bleakly. 'I don't think any of us are going to get off this rig alive.'

Six

Paul and Mark decided not to go and tell the others about their grim discovery just yet – the bad news could wait until later – instead they resumed the search for Dr Shelley on Level Two. They spent over an hour without result and then Paul suggested they go and have another look at the TV monitoring centre they'd investigated briefly the previous night.

For a time Paul fiddled with the camera controls, cutting from camera to camera around the platform in the hope that they might spot Shelley, or *anyone*, on one of the eight monitors but all they got were views of deserted corridors and labs.

By accident they found themselves, finally, watching the other four who had obviously left the kitchen and were in one of the several recreational rooms on the bottom level. The three women were playing cards in a desultory fashion while Alex sat in front of a TV set sorting through a pile of video cassettes.

'Gives you a feeling of power, doesn't it, being able to watch someone without them knowing it,' said Mark, staring at the screen.

'I guess so,' said Paul. 'I just wish there was some kind of "erase" button we could press that would get rid of Alex.'

'You hate his guts, don't you?'

'Sure. Don't you too?'

'If there was a Guinness Book of Shits he'd be Number One,' said Mark, 'I wish we'd never got involved with him.'

'Yeah, it was a big mistake all right,' agreed Paul. 'Only Linda had the smarts to see through him from the beginning. She warned me against getting mixed up with him but I didn't listen to her.'

'He wants Linda. You realise that, I hope,' said Mark calmly.

Paul nodded. 'Yeah. And if he ever so much as touches her I'll kill him.'

'You *mean* that, don't you?' said Mark. He sounded impressed.

Paul looked at him with embarrassment. 'Sounds like something out of a bad movie, but yes, I do mean it.'

'I wish I had your guts. But I'm weak. I've always been weak but now I'm weaker than ever.'

'Hey, come on Mark. Don't be so hard on yourself. You're not weak.'

'Oh yes I am.' He gave a bitter laugh. 'And you don't know the half of it.' He grimaced suddenly and grabbed the console with both hands to steady himself.

'You okay?' asked Paul, alarmed.

'Yes,' said Mark shakily, 'just a dizzy spell. I'll be fine.'

'You should really see a doctor when we get home. I think there's something wrong with you.'

He laughed again. 'You can say that again. But don't worry. I know what it is. I can handle it. But don't ask me to explain. There's nothing you can do to help. Okay?'

'Okay,' said Paul reluctantly. 'At least you're looking better today than you were yesterday. You looked awful.'

'I *feel* better. And I've stopped seeing things too. For a time there I thought I was going crazy.'

Paul frowned. 'What do you mean?'

'You remember I told you about the stuff I found in the overalls up on the crane. The black slime?'

'Yeah.'

'Well, I never finished telling you the whole story. It *moved*,

Paul. It poured out of one of the sleeves, ran across the floor of the cabin and went out through an air vent in the back. It actually crawled *up* the back wall of the cabin to reach the vent, like a kind of liquid worm . . .'

Paul stared at him. 'Are you having me on?'

'No, I swear it Paul. That's what I saw. Or that's what I *thought* I saw. Of course it must have been a hallucination. I know that now but it really shook me at the time.'

'Yeah,' said Paul, remembering how shaken he'd looked when he'd come down from the crane. 'But *why* should you be having hallucinations? Or is that part of what you can't tell me about?'

Mark nodded. 'I'm afraid so.'

'Okay, have it your way,' said Paul, a little stiffly. He turned his attention back to the monitors. The girls were still playing cards but Alex was now watching the TV set, obviously having found something he liked among the video cassettes. *And knowing him it's probably pornographic*, thought Paul sourly.

But this served to remind him of the racks of video tapes he'd noticed in the control room the day before. He got up and examined them again. 'We might as well start checking this stuff,' he told Mark. 'I just wish they weren't labelled in code.'

'Take one tape at random from each rack,' suggested Mark. 'We might have some luck.'

Paul picked out a total of ten tapes and put the first one into the VCR unit that had been built into the console. After some trial-and-error pushing of buttons one of the monitor screens went momentarily blank then began displaying the words 'The Phoenix Project – Data File 22/AX/G89812'. This was followed by a visual read-out of technical information most of which Paul couldn't make head nor tail of. There *were* terms he recognised, however, such as 'recombinant DNA', and 'nucleotides' which confirmed what he had already felt certain was the purpose behind the concealed labs.

'This proves they were doing genetic engineering experiments here,' he said to Mark.

'Yes, but it still doesn't tell us what *kind* of experiment. I mean, for all we know they might have been trying to come up with a new sort of oil-slick eating bug. This place is owned by an oil company, after all.'

'But if it was all innocent and above board then why did they go to so much trouble to camouflage these labs?' asked Paul.

'Perhaps they didn't want their competitors to know about it,' suggested Mark. 'They were afraid of industrial espionage or something. There's big money in this game, you know. They *patent* these artificial bugs the same way they patent new inventions. And that might explain those armed security guards too . . .'

'Yes,' said Paul doubtfully, still staring at the screen. Then he pointed at it. 'There's that word again – *Phoenix*. That's definitely the code name for whatever it was they were trying to make . . .'

'Phoenix. The mythical bird of fire that was reborn from its own ashes,' said Mark, and suddenly grinned. 'You think maybe they were trying to create a new line in poultry? A chicken that lays square eggs? A chicken that comes automatically covered in a crisp golden batter and in its own cardboard box?'

'Very funny,' said Paul, scowling. He pressed the 'Fast Forward' button and raced the tape quickly through to its finish. Then he tried another one. It was the same as the first – a visual record of highly specialised scientific data that neither of them could follow.

It wasn't until they tried the fifth tape that they got something different.

'Hey, that's Shelley,' cried Mark.

It *was* Dr Shelley, looking much the same as he had the previous night. He was talking directly into the camera and from the background they could see that he had made the tape in this very room. Then Paul noticed, for the first time, a small video camera above the console which was almost directly facing him.

'Turn it up,' urged Mark, 'Let's hear what he's saying.' Paul found the volume control. Suddenly Shelley's voice filled the room: ... 'and so I must admit that my initial confidence in our resuming control of the situation seems to have been misplaced. Subsequent events have proved correct the misgivings of Doctors Soames, Jameson and Englefields about our ability to subdue "Charlie". Or should we refer to it as *Phoenix*?' He shook his head wearily. 'In a sense it is the Phoenix unit that is behind all this ...'

He paused and groaned as if in pain. Then he closed his eyes and began to rub the sides of his temples. Eventually he continued, 'I feel so *tired*. But then we all do. No one has dared to sleep for the last forty-eight hours now. *It* can move so fast ... We've lost eleven more people since this morning alone. At this rate how much longer will it be before it gets *all* of us? Durkins, of course, still wants us to call for help but I definitely agree with the others on this – *it* must be kept isolated at all costs. We cannot risk offering it the means to reach the outside world. Though what will happen if it does destroy us all doesn't bear thinking about ...

'But so far everything we have tried has failed. It appears to be invulnerable, thanks to us. Fire, bullets, electricity, poison, acid, all have proved futile. We were too successful. We have created the ultimate survivor – and the ultimate destroyer. What was supposed to have been a boon to mankind has become a terrible threat. Possibly the most terrible threat it has ever faced. We *must* overcome it.'

Then the screen went blank.

Paul and Mark looked at each other. 'What do you make of *that*?' asked Mark.

Paul said slowly, 'I think we can forget about bugs designed to eat oil-slicks. Whatever they made here was in a different league altogether.' He thumped his fist on the console top. 'If only he'd said *what* it was!'

'Run the tape on further. There might be something else.'

There was. Shelley reappeared on the screen. He seemed to have aged a great deal during the intervening period. His face was drawn and haggard and there was a bruise over his right eye. He now looked very different to the man they'd seen in the lab last night, which made Paul wonder again just how much time had elapsed since the events Shelley was describing had taken place.

Shelley's voice was weaker too. 'This may be the last chance I get to use this machine. There are only a few of us left now. Dr Soames, Durkins, a couple of the guards, and it can only be a matter of time before *it* achieves complete victory. Durkins was right. We should have tried to send out a warning before it was too late but the transmitter has been destroyed. *It* is much more intelligent now but that's not surprising under the circumstances . . .'

He stopped suddenly and looked away from the camera towards, presumably, the door. He had obviously heard something. As he turned they got a brief glimpse of a pistol he was holding.

After a while he relaxed and faced the camera again. 'I'm determined it won't take me alive. I'll use this on myself first . . .' He brandished the gun at the camera. 'But even so I fear that being dead may not be protection against . . . against . . .' He swallowed noisily and didn't finish the sentence. For a few moments his self-control deserted him and they saw the face of a man who was profoundly terrified. Paul felt a wave of unease sweep over him as he stared at Shelley's face. What could it be that could scare a man so badly? That scared him even more than dying?

Shelley regained control of himself with a visible effort. 'My only hope is that someone finds these records before it's too late. I'll have to hide them somewhere so that *it* can't get them and yet where they'll be found by whoever comes here next. But *where?*'

There was a noise off-screen and Shelley spun round again. The door had apparently opened. They saw him raise the gun then heard him say, still facing away from the camera 'Oh, it's *you*, thank God . . . for a moment I thought it was . . .'

The screen went blank again.

Paul kept the tape running but there was nothing else on it. Shelley didn't reappear.

'Think there's any chance of repairing one of those boats?' asked Mark quietly.

'Take it easy. We saw Shelley last night so he obviously survived. And he certainly looked in better shape then than he did on that tape. Whatever *it* was, or is, must have been overcome by Shelley and his pals.'

'You want to make a bet on that?' said Mark. 'And what was all that stuff about being dead not a protection. Protection against *what*, that's what I want to know.'

Paul gestured at the racks of tape. 'The answer has to be there somewhere. We keep searching.'

'Hey!' Mark was staring at one of the monitors. 'Look!'

Paul looked and saw the figure of a woman walking down a corridor with her back to the camera. He glanced immediately at the screen showing the view of the recreation room and saw that all three girls were still playing cards. His pulse quickened. So there *was* someone else on the rig apart from Shelley.

'Which level is that picture coming from?' he asked excitedly. 'Can you tell?'

Mark shook his head. 'They all look alike to me.'

The woman, who was walking with a fast, purposeful stride, reached the end of the corridor and disappeared from view. Paul swore and started pressing buttons on the camera controls, hoping to pick her up on another screen. Finally he succeeded, but again she had her back to them and was rapidly moving away from the camera. This time, however, they could make out a sign on a nearby wall. It read 'Level Two'.

'She's on *this* floor,' cried Paul, leaping up. 'I'm going to find her. You try and keep track of her with the cameras in case I lose her.'

Paul hurried out of the room. Mark opened his mouth to call after him but realised he had no idea what he wanted to say. All he knew was that he didn't care for suddenly being on his own . . .

He scanned the bank of monitors for the woman. There was no sign of her so he started punching buttons at random, cutting to new cameras. Then he spotted her again. This time she was walking towards the camera. She was wearing a white lab coat and had short blonde hair but he couldn't make out her face.

Mark frowned as he stared hard at the screen. The woman was getting closer now but her face remained indistinct. Blurred even. Was there something wrong with the camera? A smear on the lens perhaps?

The woman continued to approach the camera. Then she was directly under it . . .

Mark screamed.

As the woman had walked by the camera she had looked briefly up at it. There had been no way for Mark to avoid the horrible truth . . .

She had no face.

She had eyes. The round, staring eyes of a fish. Eyes straight out of a nightmare. But that was all. The rest of her face was completely smooth.

Paul caught a glimpse of her ahead of him as she turned a corner. 'Hey!' he called and started walking faster. He hurried round the corner and saw that she was now only ten yards or so in front of him. He called out again but she didn't give any indication of hearing him. She continued on at her same fast pace.

Paul broke into a run and caught up with her just before she reached the next corner. 'Hey, I want to speak to you,' he said, grabbing her by the shoulder and pulling her around.

Then he gave a gasp of surprise.

Seven

Mark groaned. Someone was shaking him roughly by the shoulder and he wished they wouldn't. Reluctantly he opened his eyes. Where was he? Oh yes, on the floor of the video room. But why? What had happened?

He focused his eyes and saw Paul bending over him with a concerned expression. Behind him there was someone else. A woman in a white coat. With short blonde hair . . .

Then he remembered. He screamed again. Frantically he tried to scramble to his feet. He had to get away from her – the Woman With No Face. The Woman With The Round Eyes . . .

'Mark!'

Paul's yell coincided with a stinging slap on the side of Mark's face. He stopped screaming and slumped back to the floor. He could see the woman plainly now. She had attractive green eyes, snub nose and wide, sensual mouth. She was very beautiful. He stared at her in amazement.

'Mark, what's wrong? What happened?' cried Paul.

Mark couldn't speak. He continued to stare dumbly at the woman. She was looking down at him with concern in her eyes.

She spoke. 'He's suffering from shock. I've seen it before. He needs to be kept warm.'

Mark finally managed to say something. 'Who's *she* . . . ?'

'This is Dr Carol Soames. She's who we saw on the TV screen. She's going to help us. But what happened to you? What's wrong?' asked Paul.

Mark shook his head dazedly. 'I saw . . . I saw *something*. It must have been another hallucination. I'm okay now. Help me up.'

As Paul did so he said, 'What was it this time? More black slime?'

'No, no . . . I can't describe it. Don't ask me to.' He glanced at the girl and shuddered.

'It must have been bad if it made you pass out,' said Paul worriedly, then he turned to the girl. 'You said you'd explain everything if we agreed to help you to get away from this place. As spokesman for the group I guarantee no one's going to object to your coming with us so *give* – tell us what the hell is happening out here.'

She gave the door a nervous look then sighed and sat down on one of the room's three swivel chairs. 'We don't have much time so I'm going to have to make this brief. The sooner we get going the better. Charlie is under temporary control at the moment but there's no guarantee for how long . . .'

'*Who* is Charlie?' demanded Paul.

'Charlie is a nickname we gave to . . . but I'll explain from the beginning. I gather you've heard of Lloyd J. Brinkstone?'

Paul frowned. 'No. But I know this platform is owned by the Brinkstone Company.'

'Lloyd J. Brinkstone *is* the Brinkstone Company. He's enormously wealthy – a dollar billionaire. A few years ago he reached the age where he decided he had to use some of his money to do something for the human race. In fact he decided to *save* the human race. Being a Texan he doesn't think small . . .' She smiled briefly and Mark saw that his first impression of her had been correct – she *was* very beautiful – but then he had a mental flashback to the image on the screen and nausea began to build up in his throat. It had been so *real* . . .

'For years Mr Brinkstone had been obsessed by the fear that the human race would be wiped out by a nuclear war,' she continued, 'so finally he got a group of microbiologists together – I was one of them – and told us to see if there was any way the human body could be protected against hard radiation by means of genetic engineering. Money was to be no object. We could have whatever we wanted in terms of resources, equipment and so on. The result was this place . . .' She gestured around her. 'It cost millions of dollars to convert this disused rig into a secret laboratory complex. It had to be secret because we would be using genetic engineering techniques currently proscribed by most countries. The advantage of using the platform was that we could easily quarantine the labs if anything went wrong.'

'And something *did* go wrong,' said Paul.

'I'm coming to that. The project was designated The Phoenix Project and from the beginning things went well. We made some marvellous breakthroughs and soon realised that we might actually be able to achieve what Brinkstone wanted. To be honest, most of us scientists were just humouring him at the start and looked upon the project as an opportunity to carry out experiments we couldn't do anywhere else.

'What we came up with was an artificial gene – a genetically engineered, all-purpose package of DNA capable of overriding the genetic code of the host body and enabling it to adapt suddenly to drastic changes in the environment. We called it the Phoenix unit. Basically you could describe it as a genetic repair kit. The idea was that people carrying Phoenix within their cells would survive a lethal dose of radiation because the unit would alter their metabolism accordingly. In a sense it would provide *instant* evolution . . .'

'And you actually made this new gene?' asked Mark.

'Yes. In fact that was the easy part. The difficult bit was in finding a way of incorporating it into a host body. The plan was for it to spread through a body from cell to cell like a virus but, of course, there was the problem of rejection. Like any virus the Phoenix unit set off the host organism's immune system. Somehow we had to build into Phoenix an *adaptable* set of antigens which would keep changing and not allow the host's antibodies to bind onto Phoenix and destroy it.

'This shouldn't have been an insurmountable problem as some viruses possess this ability naturally but it began to seem as if we would never solve it. We made countless versions of Phoenix and tested it on different species of animal and in every case Phoenix was either rejected or provoked the host's auto-immune system into such a violent reaction it died before Phoenix could complete its attachment to the nucleus of each cell . . .

'It began to look as if the project was going to be a failure but then, unexpectedly, we found a species where everything worked as planned. Phoenix was able to overcome the creature's simple immune system and incorporate itself into the chromosomes. This meant we would be able to study Phoenix in action and move onto the next stage, which was to devise a version suitable for use in humans. But then . . . then . . .'

A shadow passed across her face and her voice died away. Mark was reminded of the way Shelley had looked the previous night.

'Something went wrong?' prompted Paul.

'Wrong?' she repeated dazedly. 'Yes. Wrong. Very wrong.'

'This creature, the one that accepted Phoenix. What was it?'

She didn't answer. Instead she turned and stared fearfully at the door. '*It's* coming,' she whispered.

Both men automatically looked at the door. Mark couldn't hear anything but the tone of her voice made his skin crawl with atavistic fear.

'*What's* coming?' asked Paul urgently.

She stood up quickly. 'I've got to get away. You stay here. You'll be safe here. It's *me* it's after . . .' She began to hurry towards the door. Paul leapt to his feet, snatched up the M16 and followed her.

'Wait, don't go!' he cried, making a grab for her arm. What happened next was totally unexpected. The girl spun round, grabbed the M16 out of Paul's hand and then gave him a shove in the chest. It didn't look a very hard shove to Mark but to his amazement Paul literally *flew* backwards through the air. He landed on the rack of video tapes which tipped over and hit the floor with a loud noise. Fearing the worst Mark rushed to him but was relieved to see that Paul was still alive. Obviously winded by the impact he was gasping for breath. As Mark helped him to sit up he choked, 'The girl . . . stop her . . .'

But it was too late. Even as Mark turned he saw the door closing and heard a distinct *click*. He ran over to it and found, as he expected, it was locked. 'Shit!' he cried, 'she's locked us in!'

Still gasping, Paul staggered to his feet and lurched to the door. 'We've got to get out of here ... if that *thing*, Charlie or whatever it's called ... is on the loose again we've ... got to warn the girls ...'

Mark kicked at the door but it was solidly built and he knew it would be impossible to break it down. 'It's no use,' he said disgustedly, 'we're trapped in here.'

'Ba-Ba-Ba-Ba-Barbara Ann; Ba-Ba-Ba-Ba-Barbara Ann ... !'

Linda felt for the handle of the small calibre revolver that she'd thrust into the waistband of her jeans at the small of her back. The situation was looking bad. Alex was getting drunker by the minute and she knew it would only be a matter of time before he made a move against either her or Chris.

He was sitting on the couch eyeing them both in an increasingly suggestive way. The bottle of whisky that he'd unfortunately discovered in the back of a cupboard was almost empty now and he wasn't even paying any more attention to the TV set on which an incredibly graphic pornographic video film was unspooling towards an imminent, and sticky, end. Out of the corner of her eye she could see a naked woman surrounded on a bed by several men making use of her every available orifice.

Alex took another swallow out of the bottle then resumed his maddening drone: 'Ba-Ba-Ba-Ba-Barbara Ann; Ba-Ba-Ba-Ba-Barbara Ann!' His eyes moved back to Linda, travelling slowly up and down her body, lingering on the tight crotch of her jeans. She felt as if he could see through her flesh as well as her clothes; that he was penetrating deep into her most vulnerable inner places. She could feel the waves of lust radiating from him like heat from a fire. She could sense the cruelty mixed in with the animal desire; if he got his hands on her she knew he wouldn't be satisfied with just sex, he would want to hurt her too. And badly. She gave an involuntary shiver which she hoped he hadn't noticed. If only Paul and Mark would get back. Where the hell *were* they? They'd been gone all morning . . .

Even Rochelle's return might be enough to avert what was undoubtedly going to be a nasty incident. But no, she didn't really expect Rochelle to come back yet. She had left furious and in tears a half an hour ago after Alex had viciously slapped her when she'd tried to take the bottle from him. Linda knew now that she and Chris should have left with her. It was too late now. Alex would surely stop them if they made any attempt to leave.

Linda glanced at Chris. She looked pale and tense and was obviously thinking along the same lines as her. Linda wondered what to do when Alex made his inevitable move. Shoot him? She'd like to but she didn't think she'd be able to. But then perhaps she wouldn't have any choice . . . if he tried to rape either her or Chris she would *have* to shoot him. If only he would just pass out . . .

'You. C'mere. I want you . . .' He was pointing at her with the bottle.

The muscles of her stomach tightened. *Oh shit*. 'What do you want?' she asked calmly.

'Wannafuck. That's what I want.' He lurched up out of the sofa, swaying badly. She hoped he would fall but he didn't.

'Linda . . .' said Chris, in warning.

'It's okay,' she said quickly, then, smiling at him, she stood up.

'Sure I'll fuck you, Alex,' she told him sweetly, 'but you've got to promise me you'll behave. Promise me you won't hurt me – that you won't be rough. Do you promise that?'

'Uh?' He hadn't been expecting this. He stared at her suspiciously through alcohol-glazed eyes. Then he grinned suddenly, pleased with himself. 'Sure . . . sure, promise.' The lie was so transparent it would have been amusing to observe his expression in different circumstances.

'Good. Shall I undress now?' She managed to keep smiling at him.

'Uh?' he grunted, frowning again. Then, 'Yeah, take 'em off. Everything.'

She slowly undid the buttons on her shirt then pulled it open, baring her breasts. He stared at them with naked, leering hunger. All that was missing was drool falling from the corner of his mouth. She had to work hard to keep the smile on her lips.

She began pulling the shirt free of her jeans. Reaching behind her she then drew the gun out of her waistband . . .

There was a crash as the bottle hit the floor and shattered. Alex was lurching towards her, hands reaching for her breasts. At the precise moment he touched her she hit him very hard on the side of the head with the butt of the gun. There was an unpleasant *thunk* sound and he reeled backwards, eyes wide with shock.

She hit him again – this time right in the middle of his forehead. He yelled with pain and sagged to his knees, clutching at his head with one hand and trying to grab her with the other.

She tried to hit him again – thinking at the same time that knocking someone out with a gun never looked this difficult in the movies – but somehow he caught her wrist. 'Run, Chris!' she screamed as she tried to pull free from his grip. Then she kicked him in the stomach. He gave a bellow of rage but she was able to break free. The gun, however, was sent skittering across the floor.

She made a dash for the doorway. Chris was already there ahead of her and they collided together as they went through the door. 'This way!' she cried, tugging on Chris's arm. They ran down the passageway in the direction of the kitchen where they'd eaten breakfast. She had no specific plan in mind – she just wanted to get as far away from Alex as possible.

As she ran she looked over her shoulder and saw, with a sick lurch of her stomach, that Alex was staggering out of the doorway. He was brandishing his switch-blade in one hand.

There was blood on his face but he gave no sign of being seriously hurt. *Oh shit!* she thought, *I should have shot him . . .*

They ran into the kitchen and Linda wondered if she should grab something, like a carving knife – if there was one – and make a stand there. But she quickly dismissed the idea. She didn't fancy her chances of winning a knife fight with Alex. If only half his stories were true he'd had a lot of practice at that sort of thing.

She herded Chris through the kitchen and into the next corridor. Their cabins were down there. All they could do was get in one and barricade the door. Somehow.

She pushed Chris through the first open door they came to. Checking to see that it had a key she slammed it shut and locked it. She knew Alex wasn't far behind them. She heard the sound of his footsteps as he half-ran, half-staggered along the corridor. Then there was silence, apart from their own ragged gasps for breath.

Then came a noise. An unpleasant one. Linda realised that it was the sound of Alex's knife being scraped across the door. Again and again. Then he began to speak. He no longer sounded drunk as he told them, in precise and clinical detail, what he was going to do to them both.

Chris's sobs changed to retching sounds as she deposited her partly digested breakfast onto the cabin floor.

Rochelle had no idea where she was going. Nor did she care. The right side of her face was still stinging badly from the slap Alex had given her. Her eyes were filled with tears but more from anger than the pain. *How dare that bastard hit her like that?* Who the hell did he think she was? Did he think he could treat her like trash and expect her to sit back and take it like an obedient puppy? He's just getting too damn big for his boots these days . . .

And it wasn't just the slap, it was the way he'd made it plain he wanted to lay Linda, Miss Goody-Two-Shoes herself. Right in front of her. And of course the previous night he'd had

Chris. She knew that for a fact. He hadn't admitted it yet but nor did he bother to even deny it – just grinned that smug grin of his. Okay, so during the eighteen months they'd been going together they'd both screwed around with other people – him especially – but they had an unspoken agreement not to be goddamned *blatant* about it. Well, as far as she was concerned he'd gone too far this time. Once they got back to dry land she was giving him the elbow...

It was about then that Rochelle realised she was lost. She wasn't even sure which level she was on. She knew she had gone up some stairs and passed through at least one set of automatic doors but how far exactly had she climbed? All these corridors looked the same. It was like being in a giant three-dimensional white maze.

She sighed and kept on walking. She would find the stairs and go down again. A tiny worm of worry was beginning to burrow into the edge of her mind but she tried to ignore it, turning her thoughts back to Alex again. She had never seen him that drunk before. It had been a bit frightening. But some-times he was a little frightening even when he wasn't drunk. There was a manic streak in him that scared her a little. But she was attracted to him in spite of – or perhaps *because* of – that. She knew it was unfashionable to admit such a thing these days, especially in front of a feminist like Chris, but she had always been something of a masochist when it came to lovers.

Not that she didn't give as good as she got at times, but there did seem to be something about her that dragged the psychopaths out of the woodwork. Small-time psychopaths at any rate.

She stopped her musing as she turned a corner and saw that the corridor came to an end at a pair of doors. After a moment's hesitation she went on through them and found herself in the big room containing all the empty cages and tanks. She frowned, trying to remember which level this had been on.

She walked down between the rows of cages, hoping

to find a way out at the other end. There was still a strange, eerie atmosphere in the aquarium and for the first time that morning she began to feel slightly ill at ease. Maybe it hadn't been a wise move to go off wandering on her own. The events of last night came back to her with painful clarity. The terrible sound that *thing* had made as it had tried to get into Paul and Linda's cabin . . .

Rochelle began to quicken her pace. Suddenly she wanted to get out of that room. Badly.

Then she came to an abrupt halt and gasped with astonishment.

There was a *body* in one of the fish tanks.

A dead body.

Her heart pounding, she moved closer. It was in the big tank – the one bearing the mysterious label 'Carcharodon' . . .

It was a woman. She was floating face-down near the bottom of the tank. She was wearing a white lab coat and had short blonde hair. She seemed fairly young.

Transfixed, Rochelle bent down beside the tank trying to see the girl's face. Then she recoiled in horror. The girl's mouth was open and protruding from it was a mass of black tendrils. It seemed as if some sort of plant or fungus was growing out of her. And the tendrils were *moving* in the still water.

As Rochelle continued to stare at this bizarre sight the girl in the tank turned her head and looked at her through the glass.

Eight

'How do you feel?'

'My side still hurts when I breathe in,' said Paul, wincing. 'I think I might have cracked a rib.'

They had given up trying to break the door down. Paul was leaning gingerly against the console, still looking shaken, while Mark sat there flicking the camera control switches. He was trying to find the others but wasn't having much luck. The recreation room was deserted now. They'd spotted Rochelle briefly on one of the screens but Chris, Linda and Alex seemed to have disappeared. Nor was there any sign of Dr Carol Soames. Or anything else, thank God. If, as she said, 'Charlie' was on the prowl again he was at least keeping a low profile.

'I can't get over how strong she was,' said Paul wonderingly. 'It was amazing. She threw me across the room as if I didn't weigh anything at all.'

'Shelley was stronger than normal, too. Remember the way he got loose from Alex? Whatever they're infected with affects the strength. Or maybe they're just crazy. I read somewhere that schizos can be abnormally strong at times . . .'

'She didn't seem sick or crazy,' said Paul. 'She was quite rational compared to Shelley last night.'

'Until she threw you across the room,' said Mark dryly.

'Yes . . .' He rubbed his side again. 'And I was so relieved to see her at first, once I got over the surprise of recognising her . . .'

'You mean you've met her *before?*'

'No. I'm talking about her photograph. Remember that clothing we found with the identification badge on it? That was hers.'

'Oh.' Mark nodded. 'I wondered why her name sounded familiar. I don't suppose she told you why she'd abandoned her clothes like that? Or what happened to the owners of all the other piles of clothes?'

'Afraid not,' said Paul. 'We didn't get around to that, unfortunately.'

'Unfortunately is the right word,' said Mark. Then he frowned. 'When we found her lab coat last night her identification badge was pinned to it, right?'

'Yes. I just told you I recognised her from the photo on it.'

'Well I'm sure she was *wearing* it just then. How could that be?'

Paul shrugged. 'She must have more than one. I don't see the point you're trying to make.'

'I don't know either. It just struck me as odd.' He shook his head. 'Have you come up with any new theories yet?'

'Well, from what she told us, if we can believe her, this artificial gene Phoenix must have got loose in the air or something and infected them all. She did say it was like a virus. Perhaps it drove them all mad and they attacked each other . . .'

'I suppose that's possible.' But he didn't sound too convinced.

Paul suddenly stabbed a finger at one of the monitors. 'Hey, stop right there and don't touch any more switches. We've found Alex!'

Mark looked at the screen. He could see Alex in long-shot. He was kicking and pounding at a door and appeared to be quite drunk. Then Mark saw something glinting in his hand and realised he was holding his switchblade. With a sick certainty he knew what was happening.

'Christ, the girls must be in there!'

Paul slammed his fists down with impotent fury onto the console top. 'And we can't do a fucking thing to help them!' he cried.

Rochelle backed away from the glass tank, her mind filled with disbelieving horror. *This can't be real! I'm having a nightmare! It's all that cheap shit we were smoking in Morocco . . . Any moment now I'm gonna wake up in the hotel room . . .*

But she didn't. Instead she was forced to watch as the woman emerged from under the water and began to climb out of the tank. The mass of oily black strands hung out of her mouth like a slimy beard. But the strands continued to move, twitching feebly with a life of their own.

Rochelle screamed. She'd always thought of herself as the type who would never scream, no matter what happened. It was only stupid women in stupid movies who screamed, or so she'd believed until now. But this was just too much. She couldn't handle *this* . . .

As she began screaming she turned to run. Her intention was to get out the door she'd come in. But she'd only gone two or three paces when she did something else that women in stupid movies always seemed to be doing – she slipped and fell.

There had been a small pool of water there that she hadn't noticed. As her right foot skidded in it she felt a burst of blinding pain in her ankle. She fell face-down on the floor, catching herself a hard blow on the chin. She was stunned, but only for a few seconds. She struggled to rise, looking back over her shoulder.

The woman was out of the tank now and walking slowly towards her. She was less than two yards away. The water was dripping from her white coat and her short blonde hair was plastered flat to her head. Despite her overwhelming terror a small part of Rochelle's mind registered the fact that the woman had very attractive green eyes. Sad eyes . . .

The black mass hanging out of her mouth was longer now. Even as Rochelle watched more of the stuff emerged. It looked like a monstrous black tongue.

She screamed again and pushed herself backwards. Using her heels and her elbows she slithered across the floor, away from the apparition, for several yards then scrambled to her feet and made another dash for the door. She was vaguely aware of the agony in her right ankle but her panic enabled her to ignore it.

She was a few feet from the door when her ankle simply gave way beneath her. Once again she was sent sprawling onto the hard floor. As she lay there, barely conscious, she heard the approaching footsteps of the woman behind her.

The sound of a distant scream penetrated Alex's befuddled brain. He frowned. It had sounded like Rochelle. Yeah, Rochelle. What was wrong with the silly bitch? He stood there trying to think, swaying slightly from side to side. The door in front of him was heavily marked with cuts and grooves from his knife but it remained firmly closed. He'd made a few attempts to break it down with his shoulder but got nothing but some bruises and headache for his efforts. He couldn't seem to get his body to do what he wanted . . . he felt sluggish, heavy . . . confused. *Maybe I'm drunk*, he thought.

He gave the door one last frustrated kick and began to stagger off down the passageway. Those bitches in there could wait until later. Right now he'd better go find Rochelle. *But why?* He frowned again then his face cleared. *Oh yeah, to teach her a lesson. He'd teach her a lesson first then he'd come back for the other two . . .*

'Ba-Ba-Ba-Ba-Barbara Ann! Ba-Ba-Ba-Ba-Barbara Ann . . . !'

His voice echoed up and down the corridors as he lurched along them, trying to find Rochelle. He became aware of the TV cameras pointing down at him at regular intervals from the walls. They began to seem threatening to him and he waved his knife at them as he passed. He wanted to smash them, to stab each of their single, unblinking eyes . . .

He was so absorbed with the camera that he almost bumped straight into the woman before he saw her. She was leaning against the wall, her eyes closed, as if sick. She was also soaking wet. Water was dripping from her white lab coat.

'Hey, who the fuck are you?' demanded Alex. He brandished the knife at her.

She opened her eyes and turned towards him. He realised that she was very good-looking. A real beauty, in fact. The old, familiar urges began to stir within him. He grinned at her.

'Help me,' she said in a voice that was not much more than a whisper. 'I'm not well. Help me get to my room. It's not far away.' If she noticed the knife she gave no sign of it.

He retracted the blade and put the knife in his back pocket. 'Yeah, sure, I'll help you, lady. Where's your room?' he said with exaggerated concern.

'Just along there.' She raised a limp hand and pointed.

'Okay then,' he said, trying unsuccessfully not to slur his words, 'Gimme your arm. I'll help you . . .'

She leaned against him and he almost fell over. *Shit, the bitch is heavier than she looks*, he thought with surprise. But then he got an arm around her waist and managed to hold her upright.

Together they began to stagger down the corridor, with Alex soon gasping with the strain and hoping she'd been telling the truth about her room not being far away.

Their progress was slow, much to his annoyance, but at the same time the feel of her body beneath the wet fabric of her coat excited him. She was slim and firmly muscled, just like Rochelle, and he looked forward to seeing what it was like in the flesh.

After what seemed hours she indicated that they had arrived. He man-handled her through the open door and onto the single bunk. She lay back with a groan. It took Alex a minute to get his breath then he leaned over her. 'You feelin' better?'

She opened her eyes again. 'Who are you?'

'Me? I'm Alex Rinaldo. Look, lady, you should get out of those wet clothes. You'll get sick.'

'Sick?' She grimaced. 'Yes, I'll get sick all right . . . very sick.'

'How'd you get all wet like that? You fall in a swimming pool or something?' asked Alex, vaguely curious in spite of his main preoccupation.

She didn't answer his question. Instead she said, 'You had better get away from this place Alex. As fast as you can.'

Thinking she was telling him to leave her cabin Alex immediately became more aggressive. 'Hey, lady, that's no way to talk to the guy who just helped you. You should show some gratitude.'

She sighed and closed her eyes. 'Go. Fast. As far away as you can.'

'I'm not going anywhere, lady. Not least till after I've got you out of those wet clothes and we've had some fun . . .' He grabbed the front of her lab coat with both hands and began to rip it open.

And got the shock of his life.

The coat appeared to be *attached* to her. As he pulled it open it was like peeling skin off an animal. The underside was all red and sticky and her bare flesh looked as if it had been flayed.

The woman gave a terrible scream and sat bolt upright on the bed. Alex screamed too. Then, in a panicky reflex action, he reached for the knife in his back pocket, flicked open the 6 inch blade and drove it straight into her heart.

Her body gave a galvanic shudder and she fell back. The scream became a hoarse, bubbling rattle then silence.

Already Alex had flung himself off the bed and was backing out of the doorway. For a brief moment he considered retrieving his knife but then he saw that something was oozing out of her chest around the hilt. Not blood but something that looked like black slime. A terrible stink began to fill the cabin.

He turned and fled.

Mark needed a fix. Badly. They'd been trapped in the video room for hours now and he was feeling worse with every passing minute. He couldn't breathe and the walls seemed to be closing in on him. His clothes were drenched with sweat but his skin felt cold and clammy. And that awful flesh-crawling sensation as if all his nerve ends had been rubbed with a wire brush had also started. It was all part of the now-familiar symptoms of withdrawal.

He stopped pacing back and forth and went over to the door and rattled the handle as if expecting to find that it wasn't really locked after all. Paul was watching him. 'What's the matter, Mark? Are you feeling sick again?'

With an effort Mark grinned at him. 'Me? No, I'm fine. I just want to get *out* of here.'

'So do I but there's nothing we can do until someone finds us.' Paul turned back to the monitors. The girls were still hiding in the cabin, presumably under the impression that Alex was still lurking outside. But Alex had wandered away over an hour ago and disappeared. If only Linda and Chris would come out and start looking for them ... if only they could communicate with them in some way. It was frustrating to be able to see where they were but not be able to do anything about it.

There was a bang on the door. Both he and Mark jumped, then glanced at each other. Who the hell could that be, wondered Paul. Rochelle or someone else? The mysterious 'Charlie' perhaps? Then they heard the door being unlocked. It opened.

It was Alex.

He actually looked relieved to see them. 'Hey, I've been looking everywhere for you guys. You got to come see this – '

He didn't get any further. Paul had leapt out of his chair and punched him very hard in the mouth. Alex hadn't been expecting it. He went down on his back and lay there looking up at Paul with dazed surprise. 'What the fuck . . . ?' Blood was already oozing from his split lower lip.

'We saw you,' said Paul, standing over him with clenched fists. 'We saw you trying to get to Linda and Chris, you bastard. I'm going to smash your damn head in –'

'For Chrissakes, forget that, will ya – this is *important*. I killed a woman.'

'You *what?*' Paul was stunned. 'Not Ro . . . ?'

'No, no. Some bitch in a white coat. But you got to come to look at her.' He got to his feet, 'Either I'm going crazy or she's not human. Come and see . . .'

Paul had no choice but to stifle his anger for the time being and follow him. The confrontation was going to have to be postponed.

Alex led the way down to the level below and then along a passageway. It took him awhile to get his bearings but finally he stopped outside an open doorway. 'In there,' he said, thickly. 'She's in there, on the bed.'

Paul looked inside. The cabin was empty. And so was the bed. 'She's not here,' he told Alex. 'Are you sure you've got the right room?'

Alex pushed him aside and went in. He bent down and picked something up from the floor. Paul saw that it was his switch-blade. 'It's the right room okay. And she was lying right there with *this* sticking out of her chest.'

'And you say her clothes seemed to be *part* of her, as if they were growing on her like skin?' He couldn't help sounding sceptical. Alex had described what had happened on the way down and Paul found it all too incredible to believe. It was his opinion that Alex had suffered from some alcohol-induced delusion.

By now Mark had entered the room too and was sniffing the air. 'It stinks in here,' he commented.

'Not as bad as it did,' said Alex. 'When that black slime started coming out of her chest the stink was enough to make you gag.'

'Black slime?' Mark stared at Alex with shocked eyes, then he turned to Paul. 'This smell – it's the same as in the crane cabin when I *thought* I saw that black slime come out of the overalls. Paul, maybe I wasn't seeing things.'

'What the fuck is he talking about?' demanded Alex. He was reverting back to his usual self now.

Mark described what he'd seen in the crane. Alex laughed uneasily. 'A pool of slime that moves around by itself? You're off your rocker.'

'Then so are you if you've been seeing women with their clothes growing out of their skin and who get up and walk away after you've stabbed them.'

'Someone must have moved her body,' growled Alex. 'I tell you she was dead.' He brandished the knife. 'I put this right through her heart. I didn't *mean* to, mind, it's just that she took me by surprise.'

'Yeah, we know you wouldn't really hurt a fly,' said Paul dryly as he examined the knife in Alex's hand. 'No sign of anything on the blade. No black stuff *or* blood. And no blood on the bed covers, or the floor.'

'You think it was the same woman we saw earlier?' asked Mark.

'I suppose so.' Paul began to look around the cabin. He opened a chest of drawers and pulled out a pile of folded women's clothing. 'She said it was her cabin?' he asked Alex.

'Yep. Come on, let's go search for whoever took her body away. They couldn't have got very far with her yet. She weighed a ton.'

Paul raised an eyebrow. 'She was unusually heavy?'

'Like she was packed with lead weights.'

'Must be the same one all right.' He told Alex about being flung across the video room by Dr Carol Soames.

'I don't understand any of this,' complained Alex. 'What the fuck is going on around here?'

'I think maybe I can help you guys out on that score,' said an American voice from behind them. They all spun round. Standing in the doorway was a young man in a dirty uniform. And he was holding an M16.

Nine

'He's still waiting out there. I know he is.'

'I don't think so,' said Linda. 'It's been ages since we've heard a sound. Alex is too drunk to be that sly. He's either gone or he's passed out. I'm going to open the door.'

'No!' Chris grabbed Linda's arm. 'Don't! He's out there. I can feel his vibes.'

Linda sighed. 'Chris, people stopped having "vibes" at the end of the 1960s. I'm going out. We can't stay in here forever. Besides Paul and Mark are probably back by now and looking for us.' She unhooked Chris's fingers from around her forearm and reached for the key in the door. As quietly as possible she unlocked the door and opened it a couple of inches. She peered out through the crack. No Alex. Encouraged she opened the door wider and looked out. The corridor was empty.

'Come on,' she said to Chris, 'it's all-clear.'

Chris reluctantly followed her out into the corridor. 'Where are we going?' she asked fearfully.

'Back to that recreation room we were in.'

'But *Alex* might be there!'

'We've got to take that chance. The guns are there and I won't feel safe again until I'm holding one. Anyway, if the guys are back yet that's the first place they'll go. So come on or I'll leave you here.'

'I'm coming,' said Chris hastily.

The recreation room was empty. Or so it seemed at first but as Linda bent down to pick up the revolver she'd dropped earlier when struggling with Alex she heard a noise. It came from a nearby cupboard.

Someone was in there.

Chris stifled a frightened gasp. Motioning her to keep silent, Linda approached the cupboard, the revolver cocked and ready to fire. This time she would have no compunction about shooting Alex if he made a move against her. If it *was* Alex . . .

She opened the cupboard door and immediately *something* leapt straight out at her with a piercing shriek. Linda fell backwards as she tried to avoid the claws that were ripping at her face. As she fell the gun exploded with a deafening report, sending a bullet harmlessly into the ceiling.

The shock of the report distracted Linda's attacker long enough for her to see who it was. 'Rochelle!' she cried.

Rochelle stared down at her. She was almost unrecognisable. Her eyes had the wild look of an animal and her lips were drawn back from her teeth in a feral snarl. But slowly recognition dawned on her face. 'Linda . . .' she whispered in surprise, 'thank God . . . I thought it was *her* . . .' She got up off Linda and covered her face with her hands. She started to sob. Linda was incredulous. She had never seen Rochelle like this before. Nothing ever unnerved *her*. Hell, if she could live with Alex she could take anything. Then she noticed a large wet patch on the front of Rochelle's jeans and realised, with distaste, that it was urine. Something had scared her so much she'd actually pissed in her pants.

'Rochelle, what happened to you?' asked Linda as Chris helped her up. 'And who do you mean by *her?*'

Rochelle had sunk down onto her haunches now, her face still covered. 'The woman from the . . . tank,' she said between sobs, 'she almost got me . . . I fell . . . my ankle . . . she *touched* me . . . but I got away . . . I crawled away and then I started running and running, but I kept falling over . . . and I could hear her behind me . . .'

'Shhh, listen!' said Chris urgently, holding up a hand. 'Someone's coming!'

'Who the hell are you?' demanded Paul.

The young man grinned at him and lowered the M16. 'Name's Ed Buckley. And boy, am I glad to see you guys. I can't tell you what it feels like to be with normal people again. '

Paul stared at him suspiciously. 'Well, I wouldn't exactly call *us* normal but what about you? How do we know *you're* all right?'

'Relax. I'm not like *them*. I avoided getting, uh, *infected*. I've been hiding out ever since. This is the first chance I've had to get to you.'

'And you're the only one who avoided getting infected?' asked Paul, still suspicious.

'I was lucky. For a time there were two of us.' He gestured at the room. 'Dr Soames was with me but she got careless. Then there was just me. I've been on my own for two weeks now, hiding from *them* . . . and Charlie . . .'

Paul sighed. 'Ed, who *is* Charlie? And what happened here? All we know is that it had something to do with some experiments to make an artificial gene called *Phoenix*.'

Buckley looked surprised. 'You know about Phoenix?'

'*I* fucking don't,' growled Alex, 'what the hell is this Phoenix?'

'We got part of the explanation from some video tapes,' said Paul, 'but we still don't know the full story.'

'Well,' said Buckley doubtfully, 'it's not easy to describe and I'm no scientist. I'm just a security jock.'

'But you had a general idea of what was going on here?'

'Yeah . . .'

'And you do know what Charlie is?'

'Yeah, but it's all pretty crazy. It's going to sound funny to you . . .'

'Believe me, Ed,' said Paul with heavy sarcasm, 'we could all do with a good chuckle. So *tell* us.'

A shot rang out.

For a few seconds everyone was too startled to react. Then Paul muttered, 'The girls . . .'

'It came from that direction,' cried Buckley, pointing down the corridor. 'Come on.'

A sick feeling enveloped Paul as he followed Buckley at a run. If anything had happened to Linda . . .

There was a great deal of mutual relief when the two groups were reunited in the recreation room. After Paul had been reassured that Linda was all right and that the gunshot had been an accident he brought her and Chris up-to-date on what they'd learned since they'd left that morning. Then it was Linda's turn to brief him and Mark on what had happened to them. By the time she'd finished Paul's anger towards Alex had been rekindled and he turned on him accusingly.

'You were going to *rape* her.'

Alex stared back unabashed. 'I was just foolin' around,' he said arrogantly. 'I was drunk, I guess. Then after she hit me on the head I got a little mad.'

'Is that *all?*' Paul began to advance on him. 'I should kill you.'

The switch-blade suddenly appeared in Alex's hand. 'Go ahead and try.'

'Leave him, Paul!' cried Linda. 'I'm fine. He didn't touch me. It's Rochelle we should worry about. Something worse happened to her. Tell them, Ro.'

Rochelle was still sitting on the floor, slumped against the cupboard door. She hadn't been taking any interest in what had been going on. There was a look of dazed terror in her eyes as if she was still seeing whatever it was that had scared her.

Then, on Linda's urging, she slowly described the events in the aquarium. When she'd completed her story there was an uneasy silence. Alex was first to break it. 'Must be the same bitch I ran into,' he said, 'but I didn't see anything wrong with her mouth.'

'And the same woman *we* encountered,' said Paul. 'Dr Carol Soames.' He turned to Buckley who was looking uncomfortable. 'Well?'

He shrugged. 'She's infected. With Phoenix. Just like the rest of them. It's a kind of parasite . . .' His voice trailed away.

'And everybody but you got infected with this thing, is that right?' asked Paul.

'Yeah. I told you that,' said the American.

'Ed, where *are* they all? This place is deserted. You're the third person we've seen since we arrived. Where are all these infected people hiding? And what's the reason for all the empty clothes we found?'

Buckley's discomfort grew visibly more acute. 'It's complicated,' he said. 'I'll try to explain but like I said I'm no scientist.'

'Go ahead. We're listening,' said Paul impatiently.

But now there was a look of alarm on Buckley's young face. 'Oh no, *it's* coming.' He turned towards the open doorway and raised his gun.

Paul turned too. He hadn't heard a sound. But the hairs on the back of his neck began to stand up.

'Everyone grab a weapon,' ordered Buckley crisply. 'If we put enough bullets into it we might be able to kill it.'

'Kill *what?*' demanded Alex as he frantically looked around for a gun. 'What's coming?'

Buckley ignored the question. He hurried over to the doorway and reached for the light switch. 'You all got guns yet? I'm gonna turn the lights off.'

With the exception of Rochelle, who hadn't moved, they hurriedly grabbed weapons and took cover where they could.

Paul, armed with one of the MI6s, took cover beside the couch, pulling Linda down beside him. She still had the revolver.

The room was suddenly plunged into darkness. The only source of light was from the open doorway. Buckley hurried back across the room and crouched down behind a chair near Rochelle. 'It's near, very near,' he hissed.

But the only thing Paul could hear was the thumping of his heart. His eyes were fixed on the oblong of light that was the doorway. Any moment now *it* would be outlined there . . .

'I still don't hear a fucking thing,' said Alex hoarsely. He was sprawled on the floor behind an upturned coffee table. Mark and Chris were huddled in the corner to the right of the door.

'Sshhh!' ordered Paul.

There was silence. Paul strained to hear any sound from outside but there was nothing.

'It's coming . . . it's coming . . .' whispered Buckley. 'You've got to kill it. Promise me you'll kill it no matter what happens to me. I'm finished anyway . . . I know that now . . .'

Paul was too occupied with watching the doorway to pay any attention to what Buckley was saying. His finger was locked around the trigger, ready to fire the instant the creature, Charlie or whatever, stepped into sight . . .

'It's close now . . . closer . . .' Buckley's nerve-wracking whisper went on. Then he said, 'It's *here*!'

Paul jumped, but the doorway remained empty.

Rochelle screamed.

Paul glanced sideways and froze with horror. Where Buckley had been crouched a dark *shape* was now standing. And *growing*. It was already over seven feet tall but as Paul watched the shape grew even taller.

He had no idea what was going on but he swung the barrel of the MI6 round towards the apparition. Beside him he heard Linda gasp as she caught sight of what he was seeing too. The shape had turned slightly and the dim light from the doorway illuminated part of it. Paul had never seen anything like it before.

The face, if you could call it that, was long and smooth except for two large round eyes that seemed horribly blank and lifeless. At the bottom of the 'face' there was an eruption of small, squirming tentacles which parted suddenly to reveal an impossibly wide mouth full of triangular teeth.

As the mouth opened Paul heard the same terrifying and utterly alien cry that he'd heard outside his cabin the night before. *This* was Charlie.

It was now over eight feet tall, its head almost brushing the ceiling. It had no neck. The head jutted forward from between a pair of massive shoulders from which hung thick, sinuous arms that seemed jointless and ended in two large clusters of tentacles which appeared to have *teeth* growing out of them.

Rochelle, still screaming, tried to crawl away from it. It noticed her immediately and lashed out with one of its 'arms'. Rochelle was scooped up off the floor and flung backwards against the wall. She bounced off it with a bone-jarring thud and lay unmoving at the thing's feet.

This had the effect of snapping Paul out of his frozen state. He took careful aim at the creature's head and pulled the trigger. It jerked as the bullets struck home but didn't fall. Instead it turned on Paul and, with an even more deafening screech of rage, began to advance towards him.

I'm going to die thought Paul as the creature approached him, but he kept firing and at the last moment it halted. It had been hurt, at last.

Two more guns opened up. Linda's and Alex's. Mark and Chris were rooted to the spot, unable to move. The thing bellowed with pain and lurched towards the door.

They couldn't let it get away again, thought Paul. They had to kill it! He kept his finger hard on the trigger but then realised his gun was empty.

Alex barely got out of the way of the creature as it moved towards the door. As he ducked to one side the coffee table he'd been hiding behind was smashed to pieces by one of the thing's flailing arms. Momentarily it filled the doorway with its bulk as it bent low to get through, then it was gone.

Paul wanted to throw up. His whole body was shaking with reaction. He walked slowly to the door and made sure that the creature was nowhere in sight then switched the light back on.

'Jesus,' whispered Alex, getting up off the floor. He was white. 'What was . . . ?'

'That was Charlie,' said Paul. He went over to where Rochelle lay. Linda was already beside her, feeling for a pulse.

'She's still alive, but she's been cut up pretty badly,' she told him.

He nodded. Rochelle's shirt was in tatters and he could see a number of vicious cuts on her upper chest. She'd been lucky not to have had her throat slashed open.

Now they knew what had been responsible for the ripped clothing they had found. But what had happened to the bodies? And what about the clothing that had been undamaged? There were still a lot of questions to be answered.

'We'll have to go find a first-aid kit,' he said blankly. 'I saw one in one of the bathrooms.'

Mark and Chris came over. Chris was staring around with a perplexed expression. 'I don't get it – where did the American go?' she asked.

'They were one and the same. Buckley *became* Charlie.'

Chris looked at him as if he was insane. 'What are you talking about?'

He tried to explain. 'Buckley turned *into* the creature. You know, like in the movies when Dr Jekyll turns into Mr Hyde . . .' His voice faltered. When you tried to put it into words it did sound ridiculous.

'That's impossible,' said Chris firmly.

'Yes.' He turned away from her. He didn't have the emotional energy to argue.

'It's not impossible,' said Mark dully. 'It explains what Rochelle saw, what Alex saw and what I saw too.' He shivered. 'I caught a glimpse of that woman scientist on one of the monitors. She looked kind of like that *thing* – the same sort of smooth face. And the same eyes. *Fish* eyes . . .'

Paul picked up the M16 that had been discarded by Buckley during his transformation. It felt cold. And he noticed there was no trace of Buckley's clothing on the floor. What had happened to it? He couldn't help thinking of the TV show, *The Incredible Hulk* – whenever the little guy turned into the Hulk he burst out of his clothing . . .

He suddenly felt like laughing but he knew if he started he wouldn't be able to stop.

With an effort he took a grip on himself and said calmly, 'So what we have here are a bunch of people who are infected with some synthetic gene that turns them into eight foot tall monsters. But *why?*' He felt certain there was still a lot he didn't know. And somehow he had to find it out. Their survival depended on it.

He was wondering how to go about this when the lights went out.

Ten

Shelley's mind was in a turmoil of despair. Everything was going wrong. They were losing control and *it* was getting stronger . . .

They? He gave a bitter laugh. He was practically on his own now. Oh, there was still Durkins and a couple of others but he doubted if they would last for much longer. Carol Soames had been his last strong ally but she too had given way under the strain. What on earth had she thought she was up to trying to get off the rig? Poor girl. She couldn't accept the fact that she was . . . finished. And then when that stupid young thug had stabbed her it was the final straw. To die *twice* was too much for any mind. Her last layer of sanity had been stripped away. Now she was like all the others.

He could still sense their presence, the mad ones. The ones

whose minds had collapsed almost as soon as they realised what had happened to them. The reality of their situation had been too awful for them to accept. Now they wandered around like feeble, hysterical ghosts.

Would *he* go that route too? It was possible. When the last thread of control had slipped from his grasp he would be at the mercy of *it* and then insanity would be the only refuge. If only they could have kept *it* on its leash long enough for the young intruders to get away. But Carol's violent death had ruptured something. *It* had come to the surface much more quickly and Shelley had known right away it was stronger. Much stronger.

And worse still, *it* was getting more intelligent. Was there a spill-over from all the trapped human minds? Were the insane ones actually fragmenting as individual personalities and becoming part of *it*? Whatever the answer it boded ill for all of them.

Especially the six young intruders. He doubted if he could keep *it* from them for very much longer.

Paul sat hunched over the video screen. Linda sat by the door, an M16 across her knees. They had been in the video room for several hours now. Paul was determined to find the answer if it existed at all on any of the tapes. He knew he probably didn't have long to do it. An emergency generator had cut in after the main one had failed but when it ran out of fuel it too would stop.

He sighed as he came to the end of another tape of technical gobbledegook that he couldn't follow. Perhaps he'd already passed the explanation for the events on the platform but lacked the brains to understand it.

'No luck?' asked Linda.

'Not yet. Let's keep going, baby. There aren't that many more to try.'

She gave him what he knew was meant to be a brave smile. It missed the target by miles. He felt sorry for her. She needed sleep badly. No, what she really needed was to get off this rig.

He slipped the next cassette into the machine and pressed the 'Play' button. Immediately he sat up. Shelley was on the screen again and talking excitedly.

'. . . it's terrible, of course, that we lost three good people but the scientific implications are enormous. It appears that we have been more successful than we dared hope. Now we have the task of harnessing the Phoenix for use in human beings . . .'

Shelley disappeared from the screen and was replaced by a shot of a shark swimming in a glass tank. Standing in front of the tank was Dr Carol Soames. She turned and grinned at whoever was holding the video camera. She looked very happy.

Shelley's off-screen voice continued, 'We were beginning to give up hope of ever finding a host organism that would accept Phoenix long enough for our needs. But then Dr Soames suggested we try a shark and so we had one shipped in. And, to everyone's relief, it worked! Phoenix successfully formed a bond with the shark's DNA material.

'I believe the reason for our success is linked with the unique nature of the shark's metabolism. Unchanged for millions of years it is both remarkably effective and remarkably *simple*. Thus our Phoenix prototype had less trouble insinuating itself into the nucleii of the creature's cells than it did with more sophisticated organisms.'

The camera closed in on the shark in the tank. Its blunt, vicious-looking head filled the screen. A round black eye stared out at Paul and he suddenly went cold. A horrible suspicion was growing within him.

'In these shots,' continued Shelley excitedly, 'the oxygen content of the water has been reduced to less than two per cent. In normal circumstances the shark should have died but here you can see that it's suffering no obvious ill effects. After a brief period of difficulty it *adapted* to the change in its environment . . . thanks to *Phoenix*!'

The camera was pulling back now and Paul glimpsed

a label on the front of the tank. He recognised it. It read 'Carcharodon'.

Shelley's face reappeared on the screen. 'For nine days we submitted our small great white to an increasingly rigorous series of tests and it survived them all. Then, on the morning of the tenth day, we made an astounding discovery.

'As part of the tests,' came Shelley's voice, 'we had stopped feeding "Charlie" as someone had dubbed him by then. Unwittingly, we had prompted a completely unexpected development. As part of his new survival mechanism Charlie had spontaneously created the means of *getting out of his tank* ...

'Yes, as incredible as it sounds he grew rudimentary limbs and simply climbed out. First he fed on all the other marine specimens that he had access to and then, after unsuccessfully trying to break into some of the animal cages, he went off to hunt for other prey. And unfortunately he found it.'

The camera cut from a row of empty fish tanks to the remains of what could have been either a man or a woman. A rib-cage, stripped of most of its flesh, and a partly eaten leg lay in a pool of blood in one of the corridors.

'Ugh!' cried Linda, from behind him. She was looking over his shoulder. He'd been so engrossed he hadn't even heard her come over.

'Sadly, we lost two more people before members of the security department cornered Charlie in a storeroom on level three,' continued Shelley. 'It put up a fierce resistance and had to be shot several times before it died.'

The screen now showed a group of armed security men standing around a dark shape on the floor. The camera moved forward unsteadily, as if its operator wasn't feeling too steady on his feet.

Linda exclaimed again as the carcass came into view on the screen. It was very different from the creature that had appeared in the recreation room but Paul could see similarities. And it was just as horrible in its own way. It was still recognisable as a shark but the body had been radically altered to enable it to hunt, and live, out of the water. It now had two massive hindlegs, capable of supporting it in a vertical position, and two smaller forelegs equipped with long, sharp-looking claws. The tail had virtually disappeared and the head had changed shape too with a pronounced lower jaw now clearly visible and the eyes much further forward . . .

The bizarre sight was abruptly replaced by Shelley's face. 'The remains will undergo dissection later today under my supervision. I predict even greater revelations await us. This is the first step in a truly momentous break-through for science.'

The screen went blank.

Paul looked at Linda. 'Some break-through. That's all the world needs right now – man eating sharks that can chase you up the beach if they miss you in the water. Isn't science wonderful.'

She moved closer to him and he put his arm around her. She was shivering. It was getting cold now that there wasn't sufficient power to run the heating system.

The tape didn't run on for very long before Shelley reappeared. The buoyancy of a few moments ago had vanished. He looked exhausted and his expression was grim.

'June the 14th. The time is 08.45. It's been almost forty-eight hours after my last entry on this machine and much has happened in the interim. I still find it difficult to believe but it seems that we have inadvertently created one of the most dangerous lifeforms ever to have existed on earth . . .'

Rochelle woke from a troubled sleep and found herself alone in the cabin. Where was Alex? He was supposed to be guarding her. Then she remembered – Mark had been here and there had been an argument. He was after more heroin and Alex was refusing to give it to him unless he promised him the world . . . and something else that neither wanted to discuss in front of her. But she had a good idea what it was – Chris. Alex wanted Chris again. Not that she cared what Alex wanted, or who. She was feeling too ill to care. But Mark, embarrassed, had insisted he and Alex go elsewhere to continue the haggling.

She'd gone to sleep after that but the pain from her injuries had woken her up. Linda and Chris had done a good job in cleaning and dressing her cuts but the codeine tablets she'd been given had worn off now and she hurt like hell. Even breathing was agony.

So she lay there staring at the ceiling and hoping that Alex would hurry up and return so she could send him for some more painkillers. The more she thought about him the more her anger grew. What a bastard he was. Fancy leaving her alone when that . . . that . . . she couldn't bring herself to focus her mind on the thing that had attacked her. She had banished it to the outer edges of her mind where it remained a shadowy, indistinct shape. Soon she would be able to convince herself none of it had happened, that it had all been a crazy dream.

She felt a tremor run through the bunk. According to Alex there was a bad storm raging outside and huge waves were breaking against the legs of the platform. She wondered if they would be safe. The newspapers often had stories about oil rigs being overturned in the North Sea . . .

She frowned.

Someone was watching her.

She raised her head from the pillow and looked around. She had to be imagining things. There was no one else in the small two-bunk cabin and nowhere for anyone to hide.

She relaxed again. Her mind was playing tricks on her, and no wonder. She wasn't going to feel safe until they were off this platform. She wished they'd never found it. Better to be adrift still in the North Sea than to be trapped in this creepy place . . .

Her right foot began to tingle. It was an extremely unpleasant sensation, much worse than pins-and-needles. Vaguely alarmed, she raised herself painfully on her elbows and looked.

Something was *moving* under the blanket down by her feet. Shocked, she flung the blanket to one side and froze . . .

Her right foot had disappeared.

Beyond the cuff of her jeans on her right leg there was nothing. Just empty space.

Then, as she watched transfixed with horror, her right leg slowly vanished as well, the jeans leg collapsing like a deflating inner tube.

I'm dreaming again!

The awful tingling sensation was in her left leg now as well. She saw it was covered with a black, glistening liquid and that a long tendril of the same substance ran across the floor from the end of the bunk and extended up the wall to disappear into a small ventilation grill. She remembered the woman with the black, slimy worms hanging out of her mouth . . .

No, no, I'm dreaming! This is not happening! The thought was a defiant mental scream.

She tried to sit up but the tingling feeling was in her hips and crotch now and she saw that she no longer existed below the waist – her jeans now lay empty on the bed.

An image of all the piles of empty clothes they had found flashed through her mind.

'Oh dear God,' she gasped, 'this is *real* . . .'

She tried to scream but it was too late. Her upper torso was now under attack as well.

Her shirt caved inwards and her head fell back onto the pillow. With wide, terrified eyes she stared helplessly at the ceiling, her mouth working frantically as she tried to suck air into lungs that no longer existed.

Then the substance moved over her eyes and the light faded. She waited for merciful oblivion.

It didn't come.

'. . . And after the dissection had been completed the various organs and specimens were placed in different containers while the bulk of the carcass was stored in a freezer . . .' Shelley paused and wiped his face with a wad of tissue. 'The next morning not a trace of the carcass or any of the specimens could be found. At first I suspected human intervention. Perhaps we had a spy among us who intended selling the results of our research to commercial interests?

'But then we made the discovery that all the experimental animals had disappeared too. The cages were intact but the animals had gone. We conducted a search for them, as well as the missing remains of Charlie, but found nothing.

'And then *people* started disappearing . . .

'In less than twelve hours we lost over thirty people. They seemed to simply vanish – we kept finding empty piles of clothing but no clue as to what had happened.

'Then, to our amazement, Charlie reappeared. He was different than before, and larger, but there was no mistaking him. Incredible as it seemed he had somehow come back to life. He attacked and killed several people before the security team again cornered him. Killing him was much more difficult this time but finally he succumbed – after being shot countless times . . .

'And then came an even greater shock. Even while the security men were checking the corpse it suddenly *dissolved*, turning into a pool of thick, viscous liquid which then *moved* of its own accord. It attacked one of the guards before they could get out of the way and we had a first hand demonstration of what had happened to the missing people.'

Shelley shut his eyes briefly and swallowed. He looked ill. Then he continued, 'The unfortunate man just shrivelled away before our eyes . . . he was literally absorbed by the substance. Then it flowed away at a fast rate and disappeared into one of the ventilators.'

Paul and Linda simultaneously turned away from the screen and stared at the single ventilator grill high up on the wall behind them. It was only a foot wide but suddenly what had previously been nothing but an innocent looking aperture had become ominous and threatening.

'My colleagues and I then attempted to produce a scientific explanation for what had been witnessed,' continued Shelley from the video screen. 'And after a great deal of deliberation we think we have the answer.

'It seems that the Phoenix genetic material and the Carcharodon DNA have bonded themselves into a single unit that has properties we didn't foresee. We planned for Phoenix to enable the host organism to evolve rapidly in order to survive but what we've got here is a complex of DNA and RNA molecules that don't *need* to be organised into a rigid system, as for example an animal like a cat or a dog, in order to exist. Instead this unique unit is evolving and adapting at a *cellular* level.

'In other words, unlike a conventional animal which can be described as a colony of various different types of cells with specialised functions which all work in harmony for the common good – ie, the *whole* animal – this creature consists of cells that can change their function from moment to moment, depending on exterior conditions. They rearrange the shape and structure of the colony, the animal, in order to ensure their own *individual* survival!'

Shelley paused and gave a rueful smile. 'I am reminded of the book *The Selfish Gene* by Dr Richard Dawkins in which he proposed the theory that all organisms, including human beings, are only mere vehicles to ensure the survival of the *genes* and not vice versa.

'Well, with Phoenix and the shark DNA we have created the ultimate selfish gene – and one that presents a terrible threat to us all.'

Paul pressed the Stop button and slumped back in the chair. 'My God,' he whispered.

'What shall we do?' Linda asked him anxiously.

He ran his fingers distractedly through his hair. 'Warn the others, I guess. But how do we protect ourselves against something like *that*?

'Shouldn't we run the rest of the tape? There might be more on it that we should know.'

'Okay,' he sighed. 'But then we must join the others right away.'

He started the machine again. Shelley continued talking: 'The unit also appears to possess properties that are even harder to accept. There have been several confirmed sightings of people we know to be ... uh ...' He paused, looking embarrassed, '... *dead*. As incredible as it seems we are faced with the fact that some of the victims are being, in a sense, resurrected by the organism.

'I can only theorise at this stage but I believe when the creature eats, or rather absorbs, its victims it also hi-jacks their DNA/RNA material. It appropriates this material in order to increase the range of its adaptive variables, achieving in an instant what it would take natural selection millions of years to accomplish.

'But when it absorbs the DNA/RNA from its victim's brain I think it also absorbs, and preserves, *memory* as well. And yes, it's possible that the victim's very personality, or parts of it, are also preserved within the organism, as awful as that may be to contemplate ...'

Alex returned to his cabin feeling angry and frustrated. As desperate as Mark had been for a fix he'd refused to go and tell that bitch Chris to play ball. Well, he'd change his tune pretty soon. When his craving got worse he'd be handing Chris over to him on a platter, garnish and all. And that bitch would go along with it too. She was soft – she'd do anything for that wimp even if it meant letting him get to her again. Alex knew she hated his guts but he didn't mind – it made it all the more enjoyable.

He turned on the light and put the M16 down against the side of the doorway. Rochelle was lying with her back to him, presumably asleep. *A lot of fun she was going to be,* he thought sourly. *Stupid bitch, getting herself hurt like that ...*

He was about to get into his bunk when she suddenly stirred and turned towards him.

'Hi,' she said, throwing off the blanket. To his surprise she was naked except for the surgical dressings taped across her chest above her breasts. She gave him a lascivious smile. 'I've been waiting for you.'

Eleven

'Hey, I thought you were real sick,' said Alex, scarcely able to believe his luck.

Rochelle reclined naked on the bunk, her legs apart. It was obvious what was on her mind. 'I'm feeling a lot better now. Great really.' Her voice had an odd, dreamy quality to it. 'The cuts are only superficial anyway.' She put her hand down between her legs and began to caress herself. 'But there is *one* thing I need to feel even better . . .'

A small warning bell started up in a dim recess of Alex's mind. He sensed that something was wrong. Rochelle didn't normally behave this way, even when she was horny. But the bell was immediately smothered by Alex's more pressing physical needs. When it came to sex he always acted first and asked questions, though only rarely, later. Any abnormalities in her behaviour he dismissed as a result of her traumatic experience in the recreation room.

He began to get out of his clothes. 'Baby, your troubles are over. Doctor Alex is here and in just two shakes his famous scalpel will be where it does you the most good.'

But as he stepped out of his pants her expression suddenly changed. 'No . . . no . . .' she whispered in a small frightened voice, 'I don't want to do this.'

He froze and stared down at her. 'What? What the fuck are you talking about?' He was in no mood to play silly female games at this point.

She looked frightened – terrified. 'I don't want to do this. *They're* making me, Alex. The crazy ones. They want to hurt us.'

Alex glanced around the room. 'Rochelle, have you flipped your wig completely?' he asked, getting angrier. 'We're alone in here.' Perhaps the swipe she took from that creature had shaken her brains up. Well, no matter. Crazy or not she was about to get well and truly screwed.

She got off the bunk. 'Alex . . . get out of here. Run while you have the chance,' she cried urgently. She gave him a shove towards the door. He shoved her back. 'Hey, you stupid bitch, I'm not going anywhere, and neither are you!' He forced her backwards to the bunk, his hands on her breasts, squeezing hard.

Her expression changed again. There was a look in her eyes he'd never seen before. She reached up and encircled his wrists with her fingers. 'Stay,' she breathed.

'Well, make up your fucking mind,' he muttered, confused now. What was going on? And what was that goddam awful smell that had suddenly filled the room. It was as if something dead had farted.

She smiled at him and he saw her tongue. It was black.

'Ro, what . . . ?'

Her tongue was emerging from between her lips. It seemed endless. He tried to recoil but she held him by the wrists with an unexpectedly strong grasp. He glanced down and saw that he was being held by a pair of *male* hands.

He couldn't comprehend what was happening.

'Ro . . . ?' he began imploringly. But as he opened his mouth to speak her black tongue suddenly leapt out at him and, before he could react, had forced itself between his teeth. Then it was thrusting down into the back of his throat . . .

Choking, and overwhelmed with panic, he struggled like a mad man to break free but Rochelle held him fast. More and more of the tongue forced itself into his mouth. It was like a giant worm burrowing its way down his throat. He could feel it going down his oesophagus, slimy and cold. So *cold* . . .

And as all this happened Rochelle's eyes stared into his with a dark, insane glee.

Mark could have been taken for dead the way he looked and Chris kept laying her head on his chest to listen to his heart. She expected it to be beating faintly and slowly but it was skittering like a startled rabbit.

Her eyes were sore from crying and tiredness. Why hadn't she been more forceful with him over his habit right from the beginning? Now it was too late. She knew that now. She had not really noticed the physical change in him until recently when she'd come across a photograph of them together taken a year ago. The difference from the way he looked now had come as a shock.

Perhaps she should go and tell Mark's father what was going on when they got back to England. But it would be a drastic step. Mark might never forgive her. And how would Mark's father react to the news that his only son was a junkie? He might reject him completely or even turn him over to the police – he was such a conservative, up-tight character.

But no, she decided, that was unlikely. He had had high hopes for Mark and they had still not quite gone. And he still indulged him in all sorts of ways even though Mark never showed him any gratitude. If Mark actually went to him and *asked* for his help she was sure the old man would be so pleased he'd do anything to help him. The problem was that Mark would never do that, no matter how bad things got.

She sighed. All that was in the future anyway. Right now Mark needed a fix badly. Alex had turned him down and she knew why even though Mark hadn't said so. Alex wanted *her* again. She'd do anything for Mark but the thought of letting Alex touch her again made her want to vomit. She couldn't even *think* of the things he'd made her do the previous night . . .

Yet sooner or later Mark was going to get so desperate for a fix he'd beg her to accommodate Alex. And what was she going to do then?

There was a knock at the door and she jumped. She was about to reach for the gun lying beside the bed when she heard Paul say, 'Mark, Chris, you okay?'

She relaxed and went to the door. But when she opened it and saw the looks on Paul and Linda's faces she began to feel anxious again. 'What's wrong? Has that *thing* come back?'

'No,' said Paul as he and Linda hurried inside. 'But we've found out the answer to all that's been happening and I'm afraid it's not good.'

Mark was awake now and sitting up. He looked dreadful – his eyes two dark shadows and his face haggard and covered in sweat. 'What's going on?' he asked as he watched Paul go up to the cabin's small ventilator grill and peer into it with the aid of a torch. 'Find something to block this up with,' he instructed Linda.

Mystified, Chris said, 'Are you feeling okay?'

Paul began to explain what they'd learned from Shelley's video tapes. When he finished Chris's first reaction was to laugh. 'It's fantastic. I can't believe it. You're saying this creature *absorbs* people . . . and then can *duplicate* them . . . ?'

She shook her head helplessly.

Paul said, 'I know it's all pretty wild but we've seen it happen for ourselves. Buckley turning into that creature. And when we followed that thing that tried to break into our cabin on the first night and only found Shelley, that's the reason why. It had turned *into* Shelley.'

'Shelley was this creature too?' asked Chris.

'And the beautiful Dr Soames. They're all one and the same. The way it seems to me is that this thing is like a genetic thief that goes around stealing human blue-prints. They're all mixed up together but every now and then one of the victims manages to come out on top, perhaps by sheer willpower, I don't know. And when that happens their original body reforms, but not for long . . .'

'Because the dominant power is this "Charlie" thing?' asked Mark.

'Yes. Charlie. Short for Carcharodon. A great white shark. Its DNA and the Phoenix genes that those stupid scientists created have formed a winning combination. And when *it* comes out on top it either manifests itself in a physical form based on what it used to be – that creature that replaced Buckley – or as some kind of liquid that can move around by itself.'

'The slime I saw in the crane,' breathed Mark, 'the black stuff that ran up the wall into the ...' He glanced up at the ventilator grill that Linda was blocking with a torn up pillow case. 'Now I *know* I wasn't hallucinating. But how come it didn't attack *me?*'

'I don't know,' Paul confessed, 'but we *do* know what happened to all those people, and why all those clothes were lying around.'

'But how come some of the clothes were all torn and bloody and the rest were unmarked?' asked Chris.

'Well,' said Paul slowly, 'Shelley's guess was that the thing has two *kinds* of hunger. When it's in its physical form the shark instincts take over and it wants to eat in the normal way – it wants to fill its belly – but when it's in the liquid shape it's hungry in a different way. The individual cells are hungry, not for food but new genetic material, new DNA / RNA or whatever it's called ...'

Chris remembered all those locked cabins with the piles of empty clothes inside. She automatically looked down at the gap beneath the door, half-expecting to see some sort of black slime oozing its way inside. 'There's no defence against it, is there?' She asked in a toneless voice. 'When it decides to get us it will, won't it?'

'Don't talk that way,' said Paul sharply. 'We *can* beat it. We *will* beat it.'

'Those scientists didn't.'

'They were taken by surprise,' he said quickly, 'by the time they knew what they were up against it was too late. All we have to do is set ourselves up in a way that will make it impossible for that thing to get to us. And then we wait ...'

'Wait for what?' asked Mark.

'Help. It should arrive soon. Someone in the Brinkstone

organisation must be wondering why they haven't received any word from the platform recently. It must be about two weeks by now. Or there might be a regular supply drop soon.'

'Or there might not be,' said Chris.

'Look, you don't leave over 200 people stuck out here in the North Sea without some kind of regular contact.'

'Officially these labs don't even exist,' said Mark. 'They probably go long periods between flights to and from the rig to avoid arousing suspicion.'

'Well, I don't think so,' said Paul, becoming irritated, 'but if anyone else has any suggestions on what we should do I'd love to hear them.'

No one did. Paul gave a resigned nod. 'Okay then, first we go and fill the others in on all this, then we get organised. And from now on keep alert for *anything* that moves, no matter how small.'

There was no response when Paul banged on Alex and Rochelle's door and he began to fear the worst. But then finally the door opened. To his surprise it was Rochelle, and she was naked. Then Paul got another surprise when he realized she was alone. 'Ro, where the hell is Alex?' he demanded as he entered the cabin, closely followed by the others. 'Why has he left you alone?'

She looked dazed. 'Alex?' she said, frowning. 'I don't know. He went out. He didn't come back.'

Linda was staring at her in astonishment. 'Ro, why on earth aren't you wearing anything? It's *freezing* in here. I told you to stay as warm as possible.'

'Warm?' Rochelle looked at her blankly.

Linda began picking up her clothes from the floor. 'Come on, I'll help you. Then you're going back to bed.'

Paul was already at work blocking the ventilator grill. 'That's just great,' he muttered. 'Alex is wandering round out there on his own. Serves him right if that thing gets him.'

'Good riddance,' said Chris darkly.

Mark, trying not to watch as Linda assisted Rochelle into her clothes, was sincerely hoping that Alex was all right. It wasn't Alex he was worried about, of course, it was the heroin. If he didn't get a fix soon . . .

'Mark, you and Chris stay here with Ro,' Paul told him, 'Linda and I are going to go collect the stuff we need. When we leave see if you can block the gap under the door.'

'What stuff are you going after?' Chris asked him.

'Food, tinned fruit . . . and extra weapons. Including those two home-made flame throwers we left in one of the kitchens with the rest of the guns.'

'What's the use?' asked Chris listlessly. 'If flamethrowers were any good against that thing the people who used them would still be around.'

Paul turned on her. He grabbed her by the arms and shook her violently. 'Now listen to me, Chris! That sort of crap isn't any help at all. You may be ready to give in but I'm not! I intend staying alive. So does Linda. But our chances are better if we *all* try and lick this thing together. You understand me?'

Startled, she nodded yes.

Paul let go of her. 'Good. Now everyone stay right here until we get back.'

Later, as he and Linda edged their way warily down the corridor towards the kitchen Linda said, 'That was a good speech you made to Chris back there. You almost had *me* convinced. But what do you really think our chances are?'

He was about to lie to her but decided against it. He was tired of playing the hero – the man with all the answers. The strain was getting too much. It would be a relief to share some of the burden with Linda – she was tough enough to handle it, he knew – so he told her the truth. 'Our chances are shit. That thing has been *designed* to survive. It's probably unkillable. It can adapt to take anything that's thrown at it. As Shelley said on one of those tapes – it's instant evolution. Unless . . .' He paused.

'Unless what?'

'Unless there's a way of destroying it faster than it can adapt. That's why I think the flame throwers are our best bet. If we could incinerate the whole thing fast enough it might not have enough time to develop the means of protecting itself. Or there's another possibility. If we could hit it at once with two different types of danger – say we spray it with acid and then burn it – it might be able to only adapt to *one* thing at a time. If the acid fails but the fire works or vice versa . . .'

'Yes.' She sounded doubtful. He knew what she was thinking. So her next words came as no surprise. 'But that stuff can move pretty fast, can't it?'

'Apparently.' Might as well continue being honest with her. 'According to Mark it practically shot up the side of the crane cabin.'

'So cornering it long enough to carry out some complicated manoeuvre isn't going to be easy.'

'No, not easy . . .'

They arrived at the kitchen and entered it slowly. It seemed full of potential hiding places for the creature and Paul felt very vulnerable and exposed as he moved to the centre of the room, his eyes scanning for the slightest indication of movement.

While Linda kept watch he then went and examined one of the flame-throwers. It was a jerry-rigged affair consisting of a fuel container linked to a cylinder of compressed air or some other gas. It looked as if it would be just as dangerous for the user as for whatever it was aimed at but he had no choice but to try it out.

He carried it over to the doorway. He studied the valves on the two tanks until he was satisfied he'd worked out which did what then he turned them on. There was a hiss of gas from the long nozzle he was holding. Nervously he lit a match and applied it to the invisible stream of gas. There was a flash and a blue-green flame extended from the nozzle. Taking a deep breath he aimed the nozzle through the doorway and turned the small handle at its base. A long jet of burning liquid was suddenly arcing its way some twelve feet down the corridor with a frightening roar. Caught by surprise, Paul could only stare at it in fascinated awe for several moments before he realised he was wasting precious fuel. Then, hurriedly, he switched it off.

'Horrible,' said Linda with distaste. 'That's the sort of thing only a man could invent. Imagine being able to use it on a human being.'

Small pools of burning fuel were spattered along the floor of the passageway. When he was certain they would go out harmlessly he turned and carried the device back into the room. 'We won't be using this against people. The thing we're fighting isn't human.'

'No, but it has people trapped inside it, in a sense. People who can still feel and think.'

'*Some* of the time, I guess. But they're dead really. Except that . . .' he frowned, not wanting to go on.

'Except that they don't know it. Or don't *want* to know it.' She said, and shuddered. 'They're dead and yet they're still alive in a horrible kind of way. They're trapped in a sort of purgatory.'

He could see the depth of her fear in her eyes and it alarmed him. 'Don't think about it,' he advised.

But she wouldn't leave it alone. 'Paul, promise you won't let it get me.'

Misunderstanding what she meant he said quickly, 'Of course I won't let it get near you.'

'No. I mean if it looks as if we're going to lose I want you to *kill* me first – before it can get me. I don't want to become a . . . *part* of it . . . Do you promise?'

He looked at her and swallowed hard. He would never be able to bring himself to kill her, he knew that, but he lied and said, 'Of course. I promise.' And for her added peace of mind he didn't tell her what Shelley had said about death possibly not being protection against the absorption of one's personality by the creature . . .

Later, as he was piling up a collection of supplies on one of the tables she said, 'There's something else worrying me.'

'Yes?'

'It's Mark. He said the thing, the slime in the crane, didn't attack him.'

'That's right.'

'Paul, how do we *know* he's telling the truth? What if it *did* attack him? What if he's part of that creature now? Has been all along . . . ?'

Patiently, Paul said, 'He can't be. He's been *with* us when Shelley and the others, including good old Charlie himself, have made appearances.'

'Yes, but Paul, how do we know there's only the *one* creature?'

Paul stopped what he was doing and stared at her. It was a good question.

Chris was getting worried about Rochelle. There was something disturbing about the way she was lying there, her eyes wide open and watching both of them so intently. Mark hadn't seemed to notice – he was too busy fighting a losing battle against his body's craving for that damned drug – but it was beginning to get on her nerves.

Finally she got up and went over to her. 'Ro, why don't you try and get some sleep. You've had a pretty nasty experience. You need rest. You – ' Suddenly she screamed and recoiled.

Immediately Mark leapt up, grabbing for one of the M16s. 'What's wrong? Is it here? Where is it?'

Shaking, Chris managed to regain control of herself. 'I'm sorry. It's nothing. My imagination's working overtime. I'm seeing things.'

'Seeing what?' he demanded.

She shook her head. She couldn't tell him that for a moment she could have sworn she saw *Alex's* eyes staring out from Rochelle's face . . .

Twelve

The cramps were getting worse. It felt as if there were steel hooks inside his belly, ripping and twisting through his guts. Mark wanted to fall onto the floor and curl up into a tight, screaming ball but instead he remained on the chair, bent forward almost double, hugging his stomach.

His eyes were watering and his skin was covered with goosebumps. This latter symptom of heroin withdrawal, he knew, was the origin of the term 'cold turkey'. He also knew that the muscle spasms he was experiencing would get progressively worse and eventually his legs would start kicking uncontrollably. This was the origin of yet another colourful expression – 'kicking the habit'. Finally the spasms would get so bad he would have spontaneous orgasms. Not that he'd be in any condition to enjoy them . . .

He knew all these things because once he'd become hooked on heroin he had studied up on the subject of drug addiction. What he'd learned had scared him profoundly but his dependence and need for the drug hadn't lessened. It was like going down a hill in a car with no brakes – you knew there was going to be a fatal crash at the bottom but there was no way you could get out of the car.

How much longer could he last without another fix? How much longer before the final convulsions and the descent into a coma? He didn't know. He had taken several codeine tablets which, like heroin, was a derivative of opium, and they had helped but not much. If only that last fix Alex gave him hadn't been so small. If only he could get *another* one . . .

He groaned aloud.

'Is it bad?' asked Chris.

'Of course it's bad, you cretin,' he hissed at her.

'Isn't there anything I can do?'

'Yeah. Go get me some smack. Go find Alex and get it off him. That's all you have to do . . .'

'Oh Mark, don't ask me to do that,' she cried in anguish. 'I can't go out there. I'm scared. That *thing* is waiting . . . And even if I could find Alex he wouldn't give me any heroin. Not unless I . . . I . . .'

Mark glared at her. 'Jesus Christ, I'm *dying* here. It won't kill you to give Alex what he wants from you. You've done it before. Hell, underneath it all you probably *enjoyed* it.'

Her eyes filled with tears. She wanted to hit him. Did he understand so little about her that he could actually think something like *that*? But she contained her anger. She knew he couldn't help himself. He was like an animal with its leg caught in a trap. He was snapping out at everything, even her.

'Well, are you going?' he demanded.

She shook her head helplessly. 'I *can't*, Mark.'

'Then we're through. It's all over between us,' he snarled. 'When we get out of here I never want to see you again.'

'Mark! You don't mean this . . . you don't know what you're saying!'

'Shut up,' he said coldly. 'The sound of your voice makes me sick. The *sight* of you makes me sick.'

'Mark . . .' she cried. 'Please don't do this to me . . .'

'The heroin's here,' said Rochelle.

Both Chris and Mark turned to her. Chris had thought she was asleep but now she was sitting up on the bunk and looking at them with the same spaced-out expression she had before.

'It's *here*?' asked Mark, disbelievingly.

'Under that mattress.' She pointed at the bunk Chris was sitting on. Chris immediately got up and pulled the corner of the mattress to one side. Lying there was a wide belt. Mark gave a wild cry and leapt out of the chair. He snatched up the belt and began to frantically rip open its series of pouches. Small plastic packets containing white powder fell onto the floor. He looked at them with the kind of wondrous awe that you normally only see depicted in religious paintings. It tore

Chris up to see how much power the damned drug had over him.

'I don't believe it,' said Mark, picking up a handful of the packets. 'I didn't think Alex would let these out of his sight for even a moment.'

'Better just take what you need and put the rest back in the belt,' advised Chris, casting a nervous glance at the door. If Alex chose this moment to return she didn't like to think what he'd do.

'Yeah, you're right,' said Mark. He stuffed three of the packets in his trouser pocket then refilled the pouches and put the belt back under the mattress. Then he started for the door.

Alarmed, she said, 'Where are you going?'

'To our cabin, to get the hypo and other stuff. Then I'm going to the bathroom to shoot up. I won't be long.' He began pulling the rags out from the gap under the door. 'Put these back after I've gone.'

'Mark, you shouldn't go out there. Wait until the others come back, then Paul can go with you.'

'No!' he cried angrily. 'I don't want Paul to know about this. You know that. And don't you tell him either.' He opened the door.

'You can't keep it a secret from him for much longer,' she persisted. 'He's going to find out sooner or later. Be sensible, Mark. Don't put your life at risk because of your stupid pride.'

He didn't answer. The door closed. She sighed and went and locked it. Nothing mattered to him anymore except that filthy drug – it was sickening and it was all Alex's fault. 'Damn you, Alex,' she muttered, 'Damn you to hell.'

Behind her, Alex sniggered.

Shocked, she spun round, expecting to see Alex there. But the only other person in the cabin was, of course, Rochelle. She was sitting up on the bunk still wearing that same stoned expression.

'God, you scared me just then,' Chris told her, 'You sounded exactly like Alex.' I must be cracking up, she thought.

First I think I see Alex's eyes in her face and now I'm hearing things.

Suddenly the blank look on Rochelle's face vanished and she screamed, 'Jesus, Chris! Get out of here! Run! Run! . . . Oh no . . .' Her face then contorted as if she was in pain and she started to whimper in a little girl's voice. 'Please, no, I don't want to go back into the dark again . . . I'm scared . . . let me stay in the light . . . *It's* down there . . . Oh no . . .' The blank look returned, as if a visor was going down over her face. She began to climb off the bunk.

Chris tried to restrain her. 'Hey, Ro, calm down,' she said anxiously, 'It's all right. Everything's going to be all right.'

Then she gasped as Rochelle pushed her back with a strength that was alarming. 'Ro . . . !' she cried.

Rochelle was now pulling at her clothes. The fabrics tore like paper and very soon she was naked. Then she was ripping off the dressings. Chris saw that the ugly wounds across the top of her chest had vanished. Her skin was smooth and unmarked.

Rochelle stared at her. The eyes were losing their blankness again. There was terror in them. As if they were looking up out of a deep pit. Then they changed. Chris's stomach tightened and her heart began thumping.

This time there was no mistaking it. Those were *Alex's* eyes.

'I guess you're right,' said Paul, 'we can't be sure there's only one of them.'

They were in one of the labs on the second level. Paul was hunting through the cupboards looking for the acids he wanted. Linda was keeping guard in the centre of the room, reluctantly holding the flame-thrower. The burner was lit which meant she could fire the device at the turn of a handle if the need arose.

Paul closed the cupboard door and slowly turned to her. There was an odd expression on his face, as if something unpleasant had just occurred to him.

It had. 'If there is more than one it means that *any* of us might be one of them. *You* could be.'

'Come on Paul, don't do this to me,' she pleaded. 'You *know* I'm not . . .'

'Do I? How? There's no way I can *really* be sure.'

'We've been alone a lot of the time,' she said carefully, knowing that this was a potential crisis unless she handled it correctly. 'If I was part of that thing I would have attacked you by now. I had plenty of opportunity.'

'Yes,' he said slyly, 'but you might not even know you *are* the thing. That Soames woman didn't, until towards the end. Hell, *I* might be *it* as well and not know it. That would be wild, wouldn't it? *Both* of us no longer real but neither realising it?' He started to laugh.

Linda unstrapped the flame-thrower from her back and put it down on the floor. Then she walked over to Paul. He continued to laugh and she knew it wasn't far from becoming all-out hysteria. She grabbed him by the shoulders and he flinched. The laughter stopped. With dismay she saw there was fear in his eyes. Fear of *her*.

'Listen to me, Paul,' she said quietly, 'this is *me*, Linda. I'm *real*.' She grabbed his wrists and pulled his hands towards her. 'Feel me.' She put his hands on her breasts. Then she leaned up and kissed him on the mouth.

For a long moment he didn't respond then she felt the tension begin to drain out of him. He let go of her breasts and wrapped his arms around her, hugging her. 'I'm sorry,' he said, 'I suppose I'm starting to crack up.'

'*You* can't afford to crack up,' she told him fiercely, 'we *need* you, Paul. You're the only one who's capable of getting us out alive. Without you the others are useless . . .'

But even as she spoke – even as she was feeling secure and safe in his arms, she couldn't help thinking, *is it really Paul?*

Rochelle's body was changing. It was expanding. The shoulders were getting wider and the chest bigger while at the same time her breasts were shrinking – turning into hard pectorals.

Chris couldn't move. She knew now what was happening, what *had* happened, but she was literally paralysed with fear. Like a rabbit caught in the headlights of some approaching juggernaut truck. She couldn't even scream.

The face was the worst thing. The features were melting and flowing like butter in a frying pan. Rochelle's nose grew thinner and sharper. Coarse pores formed on her cheeks and her chin became clefted and blue black. Her hair was like a million electrified snakes – wriggling, stretching, squirming as it grew longer from her scalp and changed colour, losing the dyed pink and becoming black and greasy.

The body continued to change. It was as if the thing that had been Rochelle was performing a disgusting travesty of an erotic dance before her. The skin shimmered and pulsated as if the muscles beneath were undergoing incredible contortions – but no human muscles could have made those shapes. And they were accompanied by sickening sounds. Grisly sounds. Bubbling, slurping sounds. The body was like a bag of slime searching for a new form.

Chris shut her eyes.

The sounds finally died away. A voice said, 'Hi, Chris. Good to see you again . . .'

She opened her eyes. As she feared Alex was standing there in front of her. He looked bigger, more powerful than before. The muscles bulged on his gleaming, naked body. Then she gasped as she glanced down and saw the huge jutting erection. It was so absurdly massive it was like a caricature of a penis, something that a dirty-minded schoolboy might draw on a toilet wall.

Alex gave her a malevolent grin and took a step towards her. She still couldn't move. 'Alex, don't hurt me . . . please don't hurt me,' she whispered.

His answer was to slap her so hard her jaw was almost broken by the impact. She fell backwards, her head spinning, but then a powerful hand had grabbed her by the shirt front and was hauling her upright again. Alex's face was now only inches from her and she could smell the stink of his breath. A long, black tongue darted out from between his lips and began to caress her face around her mouth. She shuddered with revulsion and tried to pull free but couldn't. She noticed then that his fingernails had been replaced with black, sharp-looking claws.

The tongue disappeared and he said, 'Of course I'm going to hurt you, you stuck-up, stupid bitch. I'm going to split you in two with *this* . . .' She felt him prod her in the groin with the impossibly huge member. 'And that's just for starters. Then, when I'm finished, I'm gonna let *it* have what's left. You're gonna end up in *here* with *me*. And I promise you babe you're not gonna find it much fun . . .'

She began to struggle, kicking out with her legs, but he simply lifted her up and flung her onto the bunk. She bounced off it and hit the wall then lay stunned.

Alex advanced on her with frightening speed. With one savage movement he ripped her clothes open from neck to crotch, his claws leaving long, thin cuts on her flesh. Then he flicked her legs apart with rough ease . . .

Chris shut her eyes and willed herself to die.

She got her wish. Alex's first violent thrust ruptured something vital deep within her. She bled to death internally in a very short time. Alex didn't even notice she was dead.

Paul was furious. 'I can't believe it!' he cried. 'Are you telling me they both just walked out of here *unarmed* after all I told them . . . ?'

Rochelle, blank-faced, nodded. 'Yeah. First Mark. Then Chris followed him.'

'But *why*? What was so important that Mark had to go out there alone?'

'I think he said something about going to the bathroom,' said Rochelle in the same unconcerned tone of voice.

'Oh, that's just *great*,' he exclaimed. 'I might as well just talk to myself from now on. I tell you all how goddam dangerous that thing is and Mark then calmly goes off to take a leak. I give up.' He sat down heavily on the bunk and slumped forward dejectedly.

'Careful,' warned Linda. She was sorting out the supplies they'd brought back and had placed the large bottle of sulphuric acid that Paul had found on the floor beside the bunk.

'How long have they been gone?' he asked Rochelle.

She frowned. 'I don't know. Not long.' Then she lay back on her bunk and closed her eyes. Paul looked at her with exasperation. She was out of it. She had been ever since her experience with the creature. The tough, hard-bitten Rochelle of old had gone. She'd pulled up the drawbridge and retreated into some deep mental cellar. Not that he blamed her – he felt like crawling into somewhere safe and womb-like himself.

'I don't like it,' said Linda. 'First Alex goes off by himself, now Mark and Chris. And *Alex* still hasn't returned . . .'

Paul took a deep breath. 'I think we can write Alex off. I'm pretty certain that thing must have him by now.' Then he stiffened as he heard a noise outside. He motioned to Linda to hand him his M16 . . .

There was a tap at the door. 'Hey, Chris, Ro . . . It's me. Open up.'

It was Mark. Paul got up, still holding the gun, and unlocked the door.

As soon as Mark came in it was obvious that something was wrong with him. He wore a dreamy, contented smile and acted as if he didn't have a care in the world.

'Oh, hi guys,' he said. Then he looked around and asked, 'Where's Chris?'

'She's not with you?' asked Paul.

'Me? No. I haven't seen her since I left here.' He sat down in a chair, still wearing the dazed grin.

'You didn't see Alex either?'

'Nope.'

'Or any sign of the creature?' persisted Paul.

'No. No one . . .'

Paul raised the barrel of the M16 and pointed it at Mark's head. 'Unless you can prove to me you haven't been taken over by that thing within thirty seconds I'm going to blow your head off.'

Mark's grin grew wider. 'Hey, man, stop pissing around.'

Paul pulled the trigger. The gun sounded very loud in the confines of the cabin. Mark screamed as the bullet burned a furrow along the side of his head, taking off the top of his right ear as it passed.

'The next one will be in the centre of your forehead,' said Paul calmly.

Mark clutched at at his ruined ear. Blood trickled down the side of his face. The smile had gone now. Behind him in the wall there was a small, smoking crater. 'Jesus, are you crazy?'

'You've got about fifteen seconds left.' Without looking at Linda Paul told her, 'Get the flame-thrower ready. Light the burner the way I showed you. As soon as I shoot him we'll burn the body before it has time to change.'

'I'm *not* that thing!' screamed Mark. 'I swear it! I'm *me*! For Christ's sake believe me, Paul!'

'No. I don't believe you,' said Paul coldly. 'The real Mark wouldn't have sat here so unconcerned about being told that Chris was out there on her own. The *real* Mark would have been all anxious and worried. He would have gone right out again to find her instead of sitting there with a stupid grin on his face.' He shook his head. 'Time's up.'

'No wait! Don't shoot!' He raised his hands in front of his face. 'It's because of the shit I just took! I just had a fix – I was high, Paul, I was *high*!'

Paul had been about to squeeze the trigger again but he hesitated. 'What are you talking about? What fix?'

Frantically, Mark pulled up his sleeves and showed his inner forearms to Paul. There were lots of old needle marks on both of them, most of them scarred over, but some were fresh. And one, surrounded by a bruise, was still weeping blood. Paul stared at them in confusion. 'What . . . ?' he began.

'Heroin, Paul. It's heroin. Alex had it. Christ, don't shoot!' Mark said quickly. 'I'm an addict. I have been for months. You said yourself I've been looking sick. That's the reason. You got to believe me.' He turned to Rochelle. 'I'm telling the truth, aren't I Ro? You tell him, Ro, *please.*'

Paul lowered the gun and looked at Rochelle. She was lying on the bunk and watching them so calmly that she could have been watching a soap opera on TV. Eventually she said blandly, 'Yeah. It's true.'

Mark then told Paul and Linda the whole story about the deal he had with Alex to smuggle heroin as well as hashish into Britain. When he had finished Paul said quietly, 'Perhaps I should have shot you after all. You know how I feel about heroin. Not only that but you exposed Linda and me to an amazing amount of risk. If we'd have been caught by the Customs we'd have got between ten and fifteen years for something we knew nothing about. I suppose then you'd have said how sorry you were.'

Mark made an anguished sound. 'Hell, I *am* sorry Paul. But you don't know what it's like being hooked this way. I couldn't say no to Alex. I had to do what he said.'

'Yeah, *sure* you did,' said Paul wearily. He got to his feet. 'Come on, you and I are going to look for Chris. You'd just better hope it's not too late to save her.' He turned to Linda. 'Do you mind staying here with Ro?'

Linda frowned. 'Can't we both come with you?'

'I don't think I can walk very far,' said Rochelle, with unusual promptness. 'I get dizzy when I stand up.'

'I think it's best she stays in bed,' said Paul. 'We'll try not to be long. And I'll leave the flame-thrower with you. I'll pick up the other one now, along with the rest of the stuff. Just make sure everything is blocked up. You'll be quite safe.'

'Well, okay,' said Linda dubiously. She didn't want to be

separated from Paul. She had the strong feeling that something bad was going to happen if they weren't together.

He saw her anxiety and came over and kissed her. 'Hey, cheer up. Everything's going to be okay.'

Neither of them noticed the ghost of a smile on Rochelle's lips as she watched them from the bunk.

Thirteen

'Damn,' muttered Linda.

The lights had been getting appreciably dimmer during the last few minutes and now suddenly they'd gone out altogether. That meant the emergency generator had run out of fuel now as well. It also meant that the others were stumbling around out there in the dark, which wasn't a pleasant thought. Or had Paul taken one of the flashlights with him? She couldn't remember.

She began to feel around for her own flashlight which she'd got ready as soon as the lights had begun to dim. As she did so she became aware of strange sounds emanating from the direction of Rochelle's bunk. It sounded as if she was having a convulsion.

'Ro!' she cried, 'what's the matter? Are you all right?'

There was no answer but the disturbing sounds continued. She found the flashlight and switched it on. Rochelle was lying with her face against the wall but her body was jerking and shuddering under the blanket. Alarmed, Linda stood up and was about to go to her when Rochelle turned towards her.

Linda froze. There, clearly visible in the beam of the torch, was *Alex*.

He flung off the blanket and sat up. Parts of Rochelle's clothing were still attached to him but even as Linda watched they melted into his skin and disappeared, like drops of water evaporating on a hot pavement.

By the time he swung his legs round off the bunk he was

completely naked and she could see an erection of gigantic proportions extending out from his crotch. It resembled a child's arm.

'Hi, Linda. I've been waiting for this for a long time,' he said, in a voice that sounded as if it was coming from a blocked drain.

With a tremendous effort of will she forced herself to stay calm. She knew if she panicked she was finished. 'Hello Alex,' she said. 'I can't say I'm pleased to see you. Where did you spring from?' But she already knew the answer to that. He'd been here all the time. As Rochelle. She wondered when the thing had got to her. And what about Chris?

He stood up, an ugly sneer on his face. She saw he was taller than before. Bigger. She couldn't help glancing at his penis, fascinated and repelled at the same time. 'Pretty impressive, huh?' he asked, gloating.

'You always were a big prick, Alex. Now you're an even bigger one.'

He began to advance on her. 'You can't fool me,' he said. 'Under that tough talk you're scared shitless.'

She backed away. 'Don't come any closer, Alex. I'm warning you.'

He grinned. 'Yeah. Warning me of what, bitch? You're helpless and you know it.'

She edged to one side, trying to keep as much space between them as possible. What could she do? Her mind raced. She weighed up her chances of making a rush for the door. Would she have time to unlock it and open it before he got to her? No. No way.

She kept talking, stalling for time. 'When did you – *it* – take Ro, Alex? When Mark and Chris left her alone awhile ago?'

He grimaced. 'Other way round. She got taken first. Then she took *me*.' A look of sick fear passed across his face, as if he was remembering something almost too horrible to contemplate, then the sneer reappeared. 'You want to talk to her? She's around here someplace. Having fucking hysterics

. . . She hasn't *adapted* like I have . . .' He sniggered.

'Sure. I'd like to talk to her,' said Linda, still continuing to edge sideways away from him. Anything to delay the inevitable.

Suddenly Rochelle's voice filled the room. 'Linda, Linda? Is that you? Help me, Linda! HELP ME!' The voice became a scream then turned into a scared whimpering that sounded so heart-rending that Linda wanted to cry too.

'Help me, Linda . . . I want to go home . . . help me . . .' the voice sobbed.

Her scalp tingling with the horror of it all Linda said hoarsely, 'I'll help you, Ro. We'll get you to a hospital. You'll be all right. But Ro, you've got to keep Alex away. Can you do that? Just for a little while at least? Can you?'

'No she can't, *bitch*,' said Alex. He was back.

Linda's bowels turned to water. She couldn't take much more of this. She had to *do* something. They were still circling each other but Alex was getting closer all the time. It wouldn't be long before . . .

She remembered the flame-thrower. But that was useless. She'd have to light the burner first. There was no chance of having enough time. Perhaps she could grab one of the guns? But where *were* they? It was so dark . . .

Stall. *Stall.* 'What about Chris?' she asked, with difficulty. Her throat was so dry she could hardly speak.

'She's in here too. Or rather *bits* of her are. Some memories. Odd thoughts. She'd been dead awhile before *it* took her. It meant her personality didn't come through intact. But *yours* will baby. I'm gonna keep you alive to the very end . . .'

She forced herself to smile. 'Going to have your cake and eat it too? That's just like you, Alex.' Inside her head it was just one big scream.

'Oh, you're a cool one, Linda. I got to hand you that,' he said with grudging admiration. 'But then you always were. A cool bitch. *Superior.* Always looking at me as if I was some sort of low-life *scum* . . .'

He suddenly darted forward, catching her off-guard. He grabbed her by the throat with one of his large hands and shoved her backwards into a corner. 'But you're not superior any more. *Are* you?' he hissed.

Gasping for breath, she said, 'No, no, Alex – ' Then she tried to hit him with the flashlight. But he caught her wrist with casual ease, blocking the blow before it could land.

'Yeah,' he said. 'Expected you to try that.' He leaned closer to her. His fetid smell washed over her, making her feel even more nauseous. 'I still haven't forgotten how you tried to brain me with that gun yesterday.' He loosened his grip on her throat and began to drag her towards one of the bunks. 'Now it's *my* turn.'

'What are you going to do?' she asked, unable to keep the fear out of her voice.

He shoved her against the bunk. 'It's what *you're* going to do, baby. Put the flashlight on the bunk so that it's pointing at me. I don't want you to miss anything. Then get on your knees.'

She knew then what he had in mind. And she remembered Ro telling her once that the thing that most annoyed her about Alex was his frequent demands for blow jobs. It was practically all he ever wanted.

As she knelt before him she said, 'Alex, I don't think I can do this. You're too big. I won't be able to open my mouth wide enough.'

'You'd better. Otherwise I'll just dislocate your jaw to make it easier for you.'

He wasn't joking, she knew. Shakily, she said, 'Okay, I'll try . . . I'll try . . .'

She took hold of him with her left hand. The skin felt rough, dry and very cold. Inhuman. With her right hand she was reaching for something else . . .

'Hurry up,' he commanded.

She opened her mouth as wide as she could, stretching her jaws until they hurt. While with her right hand she carefully removed the glass stopper.

As her lips touched the end of his member she suddenly recoiled and leapt to her feet. At the same time she flung the sulphuric acid at him. It sprayed over his upper body, most of it catching him in the face. A small amount of it splashed onto the back of her hand, burning it instantly.

Alex tottered backwards, clawing at his face. He let loose a high-pitched scream of agony and Linda knew she'd aimed right. She'd got his eyes . . .

Now to reach the door. But as she tried to duck past him he flailed out with one of his arms and she screamed as his razor-sharp nails raked down one side of her back. Then he had a handful of her shirt and was jerking her backwards off her feet.

The fabric gave way but too late to prevent her from being slammed into the wall with an impact that winded her. Alex was continuing to lash out wildly, trying to find her again. She managed to avoid a blow that would have probably broken her neck and attempted to duck by him for the second time.

She succeeded. Then she ran for the door. She got there and began feeling for the doorknob and key. It seemed to take a hundred years before she found them. She turned the key . . .

And screamed again as claws dug deep into her right shoulder. The next thing she knew she was being picked up and hurled like a sack of potatoes down the length of the cabin. She hit the far wall hard and felt something snap in her left forearm. She knew immediately it was broken.

She lay there in a heap, almost upside-down, stunned and helpless. She couldn't even move as Alex lurched across and stood menacingly over her. In the dim light from the torch she saw his face was covered with large white and yellow blisters from the acid. Both his eyes had been closed up by the burns but, incredibly, a *third* eye, a rudimentary one, glared down at her from the centre of his forehead.

'Fucking bitch,' he rumbled. 'For that I'm gonna peel your skin off in long strips and make you *eat* it.' He bent down, his huge hands reaching out for her. A sick despair filled her. She'd almost made it, but now . . .

Then, unexpectedly, he stepped back from her. He began to make a thin, wailing sound, like a terrified child, then fell to his knees in front of her and cried, 'Oh God, *it's* back! *It's* here . . . it's *hurting* me . . . No! It's *eating* me! Eating my *mind!*'

Alex screamed and covered his ruined face with his hands. Linda saw that his body was starting to pulsate, as if something inside was trying to get out . . .

He took his hands away and the single, unfinished eye stared at her imploringly. 'Linda, help me! Don't let it pull me back down *there* again! I want to stay up here, in the light! Oh Jesus, it's tearing me to *pieces* . . .'

His face started to change. The mouth closed up and vanished, as did the eye, and the head became more elongated. Whether he wanted to or not Alex was going.

Linda seized her opportunity. The thing was blind now, and presumably deaf, so she twisted round on her hands and knees and began to crawl past it towards the door. But moving at all was difficult; her body didn't want to obey her commands and the pain in her left arm was excruciating.

Finally she reached the door and stood up. She felt dizzy, as if she was about to pass out. *Do that and you're dead*, she told herself angrily.

She glanced back over her shoulder and saw that no trace of Alex remained. The creature resembled some kind of huge, fish-like foetus. Its skin was now a dead-white colour and looked wet and slimy. The head was long and very narrow and completely smooth except for the two large, round fish eyes . . .

Eyes. It had eyes again. And it was looking straight at her. It started to get up.

Linda screamed and desperately tried to open the door. It seemed to be jammed, then she realised it opened inwardly but in her panic she was trying to open it outwards.

At last she was outside. She hurled herself into the pitch

darkness of the corridor and ran for her life, not caring where she was going just as long as it was away from that *thing*.

She kept running, trying to ignore the explosion of pain in her broken arm that came with every jarring step, until she collided with the wall at the first turning in the corridor.

She bounced off it and landed hard on her backside on the floor. This caused an even greater burst of agony in her bad arm.

Idiot, she told herself. She struggled to get up again, gritting her teeth as she felt the two ends of the broken bone grind together. Then, behind her in the darkness, she heard a distinct *plip plop* sound. It was if someone was trying to run in flippers . . .

It was after her.

She ran blindly, not even sure if she was running in the right direction. For all she knew she could be heading straight towards it. But she knew that if she should run into the arms of that white, slimy horror her mind was going to snap instantly.

No, thank God. It was still behind her. She could hear the wet sounds of its footsteps.

She whimpered to herself as she ran. She held her right arm out in front – she didn't want to hit another wall. If she knocked herself off her feet again she knew it would reach her before she could get up.

On and on she ran. Her chest began to hurt with each breath. Coloured lights danced in the blackness. How long could she keep going before she collapsed from exhaustion? Was there ever going to be an end to this nightmare or was she already dead and in hell? When the yacht sunk had they all died without realising it?

One of the lights dancing in front of her eyes suddenly became brighter. Then, as it blinded her with its intensity, she skidded to a stop, confused . . . Behind came the remorseless *plip plop* footsteps of the creature.

A voice cried out, urgently, 'Linda, this way! Quickly!'

It was Paul.

She ran forward. Someone grabbed her in the darkness and pulled her to one side of the corridor. There was a roaring noise. She turned and saw Paul firing the flame-thrower at the approaching creature. A great gout of flame – so bright it hurt the eye to look at it – hurtled down the corridor and enveloped the thing.

For a moment Linda thought it was going to keep on coming but after a couple more steps the creature halted and started to scream. It was a hideous sound – as if a houseful of tomcats were being burned to death.

Paul kept the jet of burning liquid on it, advancing slowly towards it as he did so. The thing's torso was completely alight now, the white flesh sizzling and emitting a ghastly smell . . .

The awful squealing got more high-pitched and then the thing turned and tried to run. It didn't get very far. It collapsed to the floor and lay there writhing as the flames grew fiercer around it. Finally the screaming stopped and it was still.

The person holding her said, 'It's dead! We got it!' She realised it was Mark. He let go of her and joined Paul. The flame-thrower sputtered out and darkness briefly closed in but then Mark switched on a powerful flashlight and shone it over the blackened remains of the creature.

Linda wanted to cry out: *'Don't go near it! It's not dead! It's a trick!'* But she couldn't make her voice work. All she could do was lean up against the wall and fight the waves of unconsciousness that were lapping at her mind.

'Look out . . . it's still moving!' warned Paul. He and Mark took a quick step backwards. But the horror wasn't getting to its feet, as Linda feared it might be, instead it was shifting and bubbling – collapsing in upon itself. All three of them watched in silent awe as the creature's body dissolved rapidly into a pool of black slime, hissing like a leaky radiator. Then the slime began to move . . .

Towards them.

Paul switched on the flame-thrower again. The liquid fire poured out over the moving mass of slime. It recoiled but it didn't burn. Then, slowly, it formed itself into a long tendril that began to stretch out along the floor, away from them. Soon the bulk of the 'body' was trailing its way down the corridor and a short time later vanished from sight.

'Well, at least we've given it something to think about,' said Paul, shakily. 'But keep sweeping the floor with the light, Mark, in case it doubles back.' He switched the flame-thrower off and came over to her. 'Are you okay? What happened? Where are the others?'

'In hell,' she whispered. She started to fall and remembered nothing else.

Fourteen

Shelley was floating at the bottom of a black sea of infinite proportions. He was hiding. *It* was looking for him.

Shelley knew he couldn't survive for much longer. The others were all gone now. He was alone.

It was a disturbing new stage in the thing's development. As he had feared *it* was absorbing their very personalities in the same way that it had taken over their bodies. And in the process it was becoming intelligent itself. It was using their experiences, their thoughts, their memories, to build a single new mind around the original primitive shark mind. The Phoenix DNA/RNA had decided, in some unfathomable manner, to add intelligence to its already formidable range of survival tools . . .

And that single *gestalt* mind was undoubtedly evil. As a scientist Shelley didn't like to use the word 'evil' but he had no choice. It would have been bad enough with only the central shark personality involved – while not inherently evil its voracious primal drives certainly made it inimical to human beings whatever its physical manifestation – but the inclusion of that disgusting thug Alex had brought a strong, almost overwhelming element of genuine evil to the psychic stew.

Shelley shuddered mentally at the memory of the things Alex had done when he'd been in control of the group body. That poor girl ... Shelley had briefly come in contact with Alex's mind and found it indescribably loathsome. It was full of seething hatred and a desire to cause pain for pleasure. Perhaps he had led a sheltered life but it had come as a shock to him that another human being could think like that.

The horrible thing was that if the creature caught him he too would become part of that cauldron of malign emotions. Alex would become a *part* of him ...

When Linda regained consciousness she found herself in one of the kitchens. She was lying on a mattress that had been placed on a table. There were a number of emergency gas lamps around but the place was still too dark for her liking. And it was cold. Freezing ...

Paul helped her to sit up. She saw that he had put a rough splint on her arm but it hurt like crazy. And so did her back where Alex had clawed her.

'How you feeling?' he asked.

'Lousy. My arm ...'

He handed her a couple of pills and a cup of fruit juice. 'Painkillers. Take them. I set your arm as best I could but you'll probably have to have it reset when we get ashore.'

She swallowed the pills and the juice gratefully. She noted the way he'd said *when we get ashore* as if there were no doubt that they would. Good old Paul, still putting up a confident front. Mark, on the other hand, looked far from confident. He was sitting nearby with the flame-thrower beside him and trying to look in all directions. She realised they were in a very vulnerable and exposed position.

'The creature ... ?' she asked.

'Haven't seen it since the fun and games in the corridor,' said Paul. 'But as soon as you feel you can walk we'll get moving. We've decided to go up to the roof. There's still a storm going on outside but I think I'll feel safer out in the open air. Also the generators are up there. We might be able to get one of them started again if we can find any fuel. Or we might be able to rig up some kind of distress signal . . .'

'I'm ready to move now,' she said firmly. But when, with his help, she got down from the table she was overcome with dizziness. 'On second thoughts perhaps not *just* yet . . .' she said groggily.

Paul helped her to a chair. 'Wait a couple of minutes then we'll try again,' he advised. 'In the meantime you can tell us what happened to the others.'

'*It* got them . . .' she began but was interrupted by a cry from Mark.

'*No!* I won't believe it! It hasn't got Chris!' He jumped to his feet and came over, leaving the flame-thrower behind. 'I *know* she's all right. She's lost somewhere, that's all. We've got to keep looking for her . . .'

Paul grabbed him by his shirt front. 'Listen, you fool, you go and pick up that damn flame-thrower,' he said harshly. 'You're supposed to be on watch. It's stupidity like this that's killing us one by one. When are you idiots going to realise what we're *up* against.' He gave him a contemptuous shove backwards.

Mark, cowed, went and picked up the weapon. But as he did so he muttered, 'I don't care what you say – Chris is still alive. That thing hasn't got her.'

Linda said wearily, 'I think it has. I'm sorry, Mark, but that's what Alex told me . . .'

'Alex?' queried Paul.

She described what had happened after he and Mark had left her alone with Rochelle. 'It got her first, then Alex and then . . . Chris. It was with us in the cabin all the time – disguised as Ro – and we didn't realise it,' she concluded grimly.

'You mean *Alex* was with us. By the sound of it he was running the show.' He shook his head with disgust. 'I guess it's to be expected, knowing him. He probably feels right at home sharing a body with a man-eating shark. They must get on like long-lost relatives.'

'No,' said Linda. 'He *was* in control, but only temporarily.' She told him the way Alex had behaved before changing into the creature. 'It was like he was under attack. He sounded terrified. Whatever's in control of that thing now isn't Alex.'

'Good,' said Paul, 'I think I'd prefer to face a walking-talking shark than an invulnerable Alex.'

Linda shivered. 'I don't want to face *either* of them again. But did you notice, Paul, that the creature looked different? It wasn't the same as when it attacked us in the rec room.'

'Yeah. It's like it's going through some kind of metamorphosis. Apart from the temporary shape changes it's as if the original shark is still evolving . . .'

'Evolving into what?'

He grimaced. 'I hate to imagine. How do you feel now? Think you can walk? I'd like to get started.'

She got up. She still felt dizzy but she was determined not to delay them any longer. She didn't feel safe in the kitchen. She kept seeing things out of the corner of her eye – movements in the shadows. Was it her imagination, or . . . ?

'I thought we could go outside on this level and then climb up the gangway to the roof,' said Paul. 'I don't fancy going up through all five levels inside.'

Neither did she. 'But will we be able to get out? With the power off won't the automatic doors just stay closed?'

'If they're shut we'll have to shoot our way out. They're only glass.' He handed her a torch and picked up his M16. Then he said to Mark. 'Bring the flame-thrower and be ready to use it at a moment's notice . . .'

'No,' said Mark. 'I'm not coming. I'm going to keep searching for Chris.'

'Mark, get it through your head, she's *gone*,' said Paul brutally. 'Thanks to you. You left her alone to go have your damn fix and that thing got her. Well, it's too late to help her now.'

'No, don't say that!' cried Mark. 'It's not true. She's *alive*.'

'The way I feel about you right now I'd be happy to leave

you down here and let you throw your life away,' said Paul. 'But Linda and I need your help, so you're coming with us. Now *move*.'

Mark shook his head. 'No. I didn't kill her. I love Chris. I've got to find her. I know she's here somewhere . . .'

'I'm here, Mark.'

Chris stepped through the doorway. She looked dishevelled and tired but otherwise normal. Mark gave a cry of relief. 'Chris, thank God. I *knew* you were okay . . .' He dropped the flame-thrower and was about to rush forward but Paul was too fast for him. He stepped in front of him and gave him a hard blow in the solar plexus with the butt of the M16. Then, as Mark doubled over, he swung the barrel towards Chris.

'Don't come any closer!' he warned.

Chris halted. 'Hey Paul,' she said with a tired smile, 'take it easy. It's me . . .'

'Sure. And I'm Harrison Ford. We *know* the real Chris got taken by that thing. Right Linda?'

'That's what Alex said,' Linda agreed, staring at Chris with horrified fascination. It was almost impossible to believe that this wasn't Chris. She – it – looked so *real*.

'Alex was lying. You know what he's like. I got away from him but of course he'd never admit that.'

'No,' said Linda slowly. 'I think he was telling the truth. He gave details . . . said you were already dead by the time it got you . . . that only bits of your personality survived . . .'

'This is *ridiculous*,' said Chris. 'How can I convince you of the truth?' She looked imploringly at Mark who was still doubled-over, trying to recover his breath. 'Mark, make them understand. This is *me*.'

Paul raised the gun. 'I'm sorry but we can't take the chance . . .' But before he could pull the trigger Mark leapt up with a wild cry and flung himself on Paul, knocking him over. The M16 clattered to the floor. Linda saw a gleam of triumph in Chris's eyes as she started forward again.

Hoping with all her being that she was doing the right

thing Linda ran to the gun and scooped it up with her right hand. Then, resting it awkwardly on her stiff left arm, she fired blindly at Chris. Chris was less than four feet away and the stream of 5.63 bullets almost cut her in half. Her body was flung violently backwards as if pulled on invisible wires.

'No!'

The scream came from Mark. Leaving Paul he ran to Chris's body. 'You've killed her!'

But Paul was already up and after him. He managed to grab Mark before he could fling himself on Chris and pulled him away.

'That's not Chris, you idiot!' he yelled as he struggled with Mark. 'Look at her!'

From her open mouth a black, shiny tendril had emerged, rising up like the head of an inquisitive snake. Linda felt a wave of repugnance go through her as she watched.

Mark stopped struggling. He gave a low moan of despair as Chris's body began to collapse in upon itself.

'Quick!' said Paul urgently. 'Move yourselves! Before it can attack!' Hustling Mark ahead of him, Paul ran to the discarded flame-thrower and picked it up, then ordered Mark to grab a lamp and a flashlight. 'Out the other door, hurry!' he cried. 'Linda!'

For several seconds Linda watched, almost hypnotised, as the tendrils of black slime flowed out from the rapidly disintegrating shell of Chris's body. Then, as one of them began to pick up speed in her direction, she came to her senses and ran.

Again she found herself running down a dark corridor but at least this time she was not alone ...

When they'd put about fifty yards between themselves and the kitchen Paul called a halt. Panting he lit the burner on the flame-thrower then shot a brief jet of fire down the corridor behind them. The harsh red glare revealed no sign of the creature.

'Okay,' said Paul, 'now we follow my original plan. We'll try and get outside and head for the roof ...' He turned to

Linda. 'How are you feeling? Do you think you can make it?'

All Linda really wanted to do was lie down and sleep for a hundred years but she nodded and said, 'I'll be fine . . . *look out!*'

Her warning came too late. Mark brought down the heavy flashlight and Paul staggered as the blow caught him on the side of the head.

As Linda rushed to help him Mark whirled round and ran off into the darkness.

It was too much for him to bear. There was no way to avoid the truth. Chris was gone – and he was responsible. He couldn't live with that knowledge, not without a fix. A big one . . .

He headed for Alex's cabin. Paul had taken the three packets of heroin from him earlier so he was making for the remainder of the supply stored in the money belt. He hoped it was still under the mattress where he'd left it. If it wasn't he didn't know what he'd do.

He ran through the corridors without making any attempt at stealth. He didn't care about the creature. He didn't care about anything. Only the fix he was going to give himself soon. The fix that would banish all the demons that plagued him. The fix that would provide an entrance into a world where nothing mattered . . .

He found his way back to Alex's cabin almost by chance. He shone the torch briefly around the interior, stifling the painful realisation that this was where Chris had been killed by the thing, and then tore the mattress off the bunk. The money belt was still there.

Next he went to his cabin and picked up the hypodermic and spoon he'd hidden in a cupboard. His final destination was the bathroom. It was a big room with several separate shower cubicles and a long row of sinks. He set up the lamp on the shelf above the sinks and quickly prepared the heroin. He diluted some of the white powder with water in the spoon, heating it up with a cigarette lighter. Then he filled the hypodermic and rolled up his sleeve. After wrapping his belt tightly around his right arm to cut off the circulation and make the veins stand out he drove the needle into the biggest vein he could locate on his inner forearm.

He pushed the plunger all the way down then loosened the belt. Almost immediately his body was suffused with the unmistakable sensation of the heroin spreading through him – a kind of glorious numbness that blotted out everything and left nothing but a feeling of blank well-being. It was the ultimate anaesthetic . . .

Mark let his breath out in a long sigh and leaned his head back, eyes closed. Already the unbearable fact of Chris's death and his guilt over it had been reduced to a barely troublesome pinpoint in his mind. The hypodermic fell from his hand and clattered onto the floor.

The noise made him open his eyes. That's when he saw it.

He could just make it out – a long black stain on the ceiling. It stretched all the way across from a ventilator grill and ended directly above his head.

It took him awhile to work out what it was. He opened his mouth to scream but as he did so the black slime dropped down on him. It covered his head and face completely, filling his nostrils and slithering down his throat.

And as the creature invaded his body, breaking it down to its basic chemical compounds, his mind was similarly penetrated by a psychic presence that felt icy cold and unspeakably evil. Mark had a mental impression of something white and slimy lurking in the blackness that had enveloped him. Then he screamed as it began to rip and tear at his unprotected self . . .

But he was already lost in a different universe and his scream was a feeble mental flicker against an infinite ocean of darkness as the Beast consumed him . . .

'It's useless,' said Paul impatiently, 'we'll never find him. Let's go topside. We did our best.'

'But we can't just leave him,' protested Linda.

'*I* can. Besides, it's probably too late to help him by now.

We've risked our lives for him long enough. I'm tired and I'm about to drop. I want to get *out* of here.'

They had been searching for Mark for about twenty minutes. They had checked his cabin and several other rooms but without success.

'He's your best friend, Paul,' persisted Linda. 'You can't abandon him to that creature . . .'

'He *was* my best friend. Now he's a pathetic junkie who'd sell us out for just a sniff of heroin. And don't forget it was his fault the slimer got Chris.'

'I know, but . . .' she paused. Then, 'Look, up ahead. A glow.'

'I see it. It's coming from one of the bathrooms.'

They approached the doorway cautiously. What they saw inside shocked them in spite of all the bizarre things they'd witnessed during the last forty-eight hours.

'Oh God . . .' said Linda.

'Careful. Get ready to move fast,' said Paul, lighting the flame-thrower.

But the thing on the bathroom floor didn't stir. Finally Paul walked warily towards it for a closer look.

Parts of it were still recognisable as Mark – and his clothes lying nearby were further proof of his fate – but sections of several other bodies also protruded from the grotesque mass of organic material on the floor. Arms, legs, heads, the entire upper section of a female torso, as well as bits of animals too.

At first Paul thought the whole hideous mess was dead but then, to his profound disappointment, he saw one of the appendages stir. And then one of the heads – one he didn't recognise, thankfully – opened its eyes and looked at him disinterestedly. The eyes closed again . . .

'What does it mean?' asked Linda anxiously from the doorway. 'What's happening to it *now*?'

'I don't know,' said Paul helplessly. He was wondering whether it would do any good to try and incinerate it again.

Then he noticed the fallen hypodermic and the plastic packets of white powder. He picked up the hypodermic. It was empty. Mark had obviously just given himself a fix when the thing took him by surprise.

Paul stared thoughtfully at the obscene mass of slimy white flesh with its protruding sections of human and animal anatomy. A slow smile began to spread across his face. Then he actually laughed aloud.

For Linda, under the circumstances, it was an unnerving sound. 'What's the matter, Paul?' she cried. 'Are you all right?'

He grinned at her. 'I've just figured out what's up with our unpleasant friend here. Would you believe it? The bastard's *stoned* . . .'

Fifteen

Linda was home again. It was Sunday morning and she and Paul were in their small flat in Islington, North London. They had spent the morning having a luxurious lie-in and were now about to go down to the local pub with their next-door-neighbours, a young couple called Greg and Sheila who were good friends of theirs.

It was a hot day and the pub was crowded so they sat in the beer garden at the rear of the building. Linda felt very happy and contented. It was great to be back in familiar surroundings again with familiar faces. It made her feel secure.

She needed that feeling. She couldn't remember exactly what had happened but she knew it had seemed like a terrible nightmare at the time . . .

But it was all over now. Gone and forgotten. She caught Paul's eye and grinned at him. He grinned back and raised his pint of bitter. She picked up her glass too, clinked it with his then took a swallow . . .

She had to spit it out. It tasted horrible. She stared into the glass but instead of the expected scotch and lemonade it was filled with some kind of black jelly. And it was *moving*; trying to get out of the glass.

She flung the glass away and leapt to her feet. 'Paul!' she screamed.

But he remained motionless in his seat, looking at her with a blank expression. Then he opened his mouth and the same black jelly that had been in the glass began to ooze out of his mouth. She screamed again and turned to Greg and Sheila for help. But they too were undergoing the same horrible transformation. Black slime was dripping from their mouths too and their eyes were black holes leading into a pit where something nameless lurked, waiting ... waiting for *her*.

She tried to run but then she saw that *everyone* in the beer garden looked the same. And they were moving in on her. She was surrounded. Trapped. And all alone.

She shut her eyes and screamed.

'Linda!'

She was being shaken by the shoulder. It *had* her. She screamed louder.

'LINDA! It's me, *Paul*. You were having a nightmare, that's all!'

She opened her eyes. Paul was leaning over her. She was in a small room lit by a single lamp. *Where am I?* she wondered. Totally disorientated, she couldn't remember a thing at first, then it all came flooding back...

She groaned. The nightmare wasn't over. They were still on the rig.

'Linda? Are you okay?'

She sat up on the bunk. The movement made the pain in her broken arm worse. 'I think so. What time is it?'

'Almost six in the morning. I think we should get moving. I want to check the creature.'

She remembered the events of a few hours ago. They had found the creature in a comatose state in the bathroom where it had got poor Mark. Paul decided that it had been affected by the heroin that Mark had just taken before he was absorbed by the thing. Excitedly, he told her they might have accidentally discovered an effective way of dealing with it . . .

'If it was a simple poison the thing would just evolve the means of neutralising it,' he had said, 'but because it doesn't chemically perceive the heroin as a threat to its existence it's *susceptible* to it.'

'Fine,' she said impatiently, trying to avoid looking at the horror on the floor but at the same time worried that it might suddenly spring to life, 'but how does that help us? It'll just wear off eventually.'

'Not if we give it a massive *overdose!*' Paul had cried. 'Who knows – it might even kill it before it realises what's happening. At the very least it will knock it out of action for a few days and give us time to get away from here.'

So they then spent about half-an-hour dissolving the heroin in water and injecting it into the creature. Or rather Paul did all the injecting; she couldn't bring herself to go near the thing. Just being in the same room as the slimy mass with its ghastly outcrops of human and animal sections was almost too much for her.

They only used two thirds of the drug altogether. Paul decided to keep the rest in reserve. 'We'll come back in the morning. If it's dead – great! If not, we'll inject the rest of it and then make for the roof.'

'We're not going up there now?' she'd asked.

'No. I think we can risk grabbing some sleep in one of the cabins. We're both in need of some rest – you especially.'

'Are you sure we can take the chance?' she asked.

She prayed he would say yes – she couldn't imagine anything better than to be able to go to bed and sleep, even if it was only for a couple of hours.

'Yes. I think so. The small amount of junk it got from Mark's body put it under for quite a time so all this we've pumped into it should really drop it in its tracks.'

'I hope you're right,' she'd said, glancing briefly at the thing and looking away with a shiver.

And now, five hours later, she felt just as exhausted and sore as before she'd gone to sleep. And the nightmare echoed in her mind like a nasty after-taste . . .

Her first try at getting off the bunk wasn't a success. On top of everything else she was very stiff. She looked at her bare legs and groaned. They were covered with dark bruises and ugly abrasions – a legacy from her encounter with the transformed Alex. And from the feel of her back and shoulder where Alex's claws had dug into her she was an even bigger mess.

She picked up her jeans with her one good hand and began to struggle into them. As she did so she realised they stank. And so did her shirt. 'I need a bath,' she moaned.

'You need a hospital,' Paul told her. He was already dressed and was strapping the flame-thrower onto his back. She saw that the few hours sleep hadn't done him much visible good either. He still looked haggard and there were lines on his face she'd never noticed before. He was only twenty-six but now he looked thirty-six. She guessed that the terrible events of the last couple of days were going to leave indelible marks on both of them.

When she was ready Paul told her to carry the lamp. He was carrying both the flame-thrower and one of the M16s. Then they headed back to the bathroom where they'd found the creature. But when they arrived they got a shock.

It was gone.

The floor was bare. All that was left was Mark's pathetic pile of empty clothing.

'Oh no,' groaned Linda. This meant the horror would continue. It *was* a nightmare. It would go on and on . . .

'I don't believe it,' said Paul angrily. 'We injected enough heroin into it to drop a herd of elephants.'

'It must have adapted to the drug after all. It sensed it was a form of poison and the Phoenix gene devised a protection against it . . .'

Paul sighed. 'You're probably right. The damn thing just *can't* be killed.'

'What do we do now?' she asked, nervously glancing behind her.

'We head straight for the roof. Come on.'

The nightmare feeling grew more pronounced as Linda followed him down the black corridor. It seemed they had been running from the creature for years – for an eternity. Would it never end? Or would they suffer the same fate as all the others? Was it simply playing with them? Like a sadistic little boy pulling the wings off a fly?

Then came a bad moment when Paul admitted he was lost. But to her relief he quickly got his bearings again and sounded confident that they were moving in the right direction again.

'Not much further now,' he told her. 'The airlock leading to the outside door should be in the next corridor.'

'Good,' she said. It would be marvellous to breathe fresh air again. Since the power had cut off the atmosphere had become increasingly stale.

They were just turning into the corridor that led to the airlock when a nearby door suddenly opened and a man emerged. He was dressed in some sort of overalls and carrying a flashlight. Linda screamed.

Paul's reaction was immediate. He spun round to face him, raising the barrel of the M16 at the same time. The man had taken only one step through the doorway when Paul fired.

It was a replay of what had happened when Linda had shot 'Chris'. The fusillade of bullets at such close range blasted the man backwards off his feet and he disappeared into the darkness beyond the doorway.

Not pausing to check the body Paul cried urgently, 'Quickly! Get moving before it has time to change!'

They ran down the corridor and, to Linda's joy, the light from their lamp revealed the entrance to the airlock. And even better, the glass doors were open.

Then, unbelievably, they were opening the outer door and

stepping through onto a catwalk outside. Linda blinked in confusion as her senses were abruptly assaulted by a combination of grey light, cold wind and wet rain. She stared at the heaving sea in fascination, as if she'd never seen it before.

'The worst of the storm has passed, thank God,' said Paul, having to shout against the wind. 'But that swell is pretty bad . . .'

Linda nodded. The sea was rising up the massive platform leg directly below them until it almost reached the catwalk on which they stood, before dropping away a considerable distance. She guessed it was a difference of some thirty or forty feet between the sea's peaks and the troughs.

'We've got a long climb to the top,' yelled Paul. 'You think you can manage it now?'

'Yes,' she said, turning off the lamp and hooking it onto her belt, 'Let's go . . .'

'You go first,' he told her, 'and be careful. The steps will be as slippery as hell.'

He was right. Climbing up the steep gangways with only one arm to hang on with was difficult and she almost fell several times on the wet metal steps which were as smooth as ice.

Paul had problems too, having to carry both the flame-thrower and the M16, but finally they made it to the second level from the top. Linda knew she would never be able to climb the ladder that led to the roof but then Paul discovered another gangway. It went up to the helicopter landing pad directly overhead.

'We should be able to cross from there onto the roof,' said Paul. 'First we'll get you set up under shelter somewhere then I'll scout around the life boats and emergency lockers and see what I can find in the way of flares and stuff . . .'

Linda was wet through and frozen to the bone when she at last emerged onto the helicopter pad. But then all thought of her acute discomfort fled from her mind.

Sitting there on the pad was a large helicopter.

It was painted bright yellow with the Brinkstone insignia on its side.

'Oh Paul!' she cried, 'We're saved! We're saved!'

Paul had hauled himself up the last few steps of the gangway and was standing beside her, staring open-mouthed at the aircraft. For a moment he looked profoundly relieved, then his expression turned grim.

'What's the matter?' she asked, 'Can't you see? We've been rescued!' Then, leaving him, she ran across the platform to the big machine and peered in through the large open door in its side. To her disappointment it was empty.

'No one here,' she called to Paul as he approached. He was looking even grimmer.

'I wish I knew how to fly one of these things,' he said.

She frowned at him. She couldn't understand why he was reacting so strangely to their being rescued. 'Why? You don't have to. The pilot will fly it.'

'The man down below. That was the pilot, Linda. And I killed him.'

Sixteen

Linda refused to believe it. 'No! That wasn't the pilot! You shot the creature!'

'I wish I had,' said Paul bitterly. 'But think back – the guy was carrying a flashlight. The thing wouldn't do that. And that's why the airlock was open. He'd just come in from outside.' He shook his head. 'No. That was a real person I shot down there. I've just committed a murder . . .'

'But you didn't *know* . . . and we can't be sure yet that was the pilot. You could be wrong.' *Please* say you're wrong, she pleaded silently. To be this close to rescue and then have their hopes dashed was ridiculous. It couldn't happen. It was too *cruel*.

Paul didn't answer. He climbed into the machine and began

to investigate its interior. She stood there helplessly, feeling the cold wind pluck at her tattered shirt with icy fingers. She had never experienced despair as overwhelming as this before. For a moment she contemplated going to the edge of the pad and throwing herself over the side.

'It's a Sikorsky S-76,' came Paul's voice from inside the helicopter. 'It's pretty new too. These things haven't been in service long. It's supposed to be a good aircraft.'

'Well, that *is* fascinating,' she said with heavy sarcasm. Then she decided to follow him into the machine. At least it would be warmer in there. 'You know everything Paul,' she said as she climbed in. 'Are you *sure* you wouldn't be able to fly this thing? Maybe you could get us as far as another oil platform? We could ditch in the sea beside it. Just as long as we could get away from *here*.'

If he noticed her sarcasm he didn't give any sign of it. 'I know the basics of flying a helicopter,' he replied seriously, 'but that's light years away from actually being able to fly one. They're difficult things to handle, even for experienced pilots. If the weather conditions were perfect I might succeed in lifting her off the pad without smashing the tail rotor to pieces but I wouldn't bet on it. In *this* wind – forget it.'

'So what are we going to do?' she demanded.

'I don't know,' he said blandly. She didn't like the sound of his voice. It gave the impression that he'd given up at last. She watched worriedly as he climbed forward into one of the pilot's seats and started examining the control panel as if he was looking over a new car in a showroom. How long would it be, she wondered, before that thing followed them up here?

She moved closer to Paul, peering over his shoulder at the maze of different instruments in front of him. Then she noticed something that sent a pulse of excitement through her. When he'd sat down he'd picked up a pilot's helmet from the seat and shifted it to the other one. Now there were *two* helmets resting on the other seat.

She dug her fingers into Paul's shoulder. 'Paul, there are two of them! Two pilots! See, the helmets!'

He looked at them for a long time and then turned to her. His eyes were alive again. 'Christ, you're right!' he exclaimed. He started to get up. 'We've got to find the other one, fast. Before *it* gets him . . .'

'Go back in there again?' she cried. The thought of entering those dark corridors made her stomach muscles contract unpleasantly. 'No, I can't. Don't ask me to.'

'Okay. You wait here.' He pushed past her and jumped down onto the pad.

'Wait!'

He stood there impatiently. 'Well, are you coming or not?'

She didn't know what to do. She didn't want to go back inside again but neither did she want to be left on her own. She had the strong feeling that if she let Paul out of her sight she'd never see him alive again. Oh, she might see something that *looked* like Paul but how would she know for certain it was him?

She took a deep breath. 'Okay,' she said reluctantly. 'I'll come with you.'

'Hurry then.' He helped her out of the helicopter then headed for the gangway.

'We'll go in the door we first entered on the top level,' he told her as they climbed down. 'I imagine they must have split up. One went to the bottom level and the other one probably worked his way down from the top.'

As they entered the passageway Paul's theory seemed correct because the airlock was standing open here too. They hurried through the corridors but could find no trace of the pilot.

'He must already be down on one of the lower levels,' panted Paul.

Of course he must be, thought Linda sourly, her heart thumping from both exertion and fear. It was too much to expect that they would locate him straight away without any trouble. The platform wasn't going to let them go *that* easily.

But they didn't find him on the second level either.

They went down to the next one . . . and immediately came face to face with Shelley.

They almost collided with him as they turned a corner. He was staggering along in a kind of drunk's shuffle. When he saw them he slumped against the wall and raised a hand. 'No, don't shoot! You must listen to me . . .'

Paul was already aiming the M16. But he held his fire. Linda guessed that after his accidental shooting of the pilot he was going to have difficulty in using the gun again, even against the creature.

'Don't waste your time talking,' he snarled, 'you're not Shelley. This is just another of *your* tricks. You're Charlie or Phoenix or whatever and I'm going to blow your head off . . .'

'It's no trick!' cried Shelley. 'I'm still *me* . . . I'm the last one left in here with my own personality intact . . . but I don't know how much longer I can hold out. You must listen to what I have to say, it's vitally important . . .'

'I don't believe you,' said Paul. But he didn't shoot.

'It's *dying*,' gasped Shelley. 'You have succeeded where I and all my colleagues, with our scientific resources, failed. You have found a way to destroy the Phoenix . . .'

'What do you mean?' asked Paul suspiciously.

Shelley was barely able to stand upright. His limbs were shaking and his face had the pallor of a man in the last stages of a terminal illness. Linda was reminded of the way Mark had looked before . . .

'The heroin,' said Shelley. 'Your idea to inject the creature with heroin was a master-stroke . . .'

'But it didn't kill it. It's still . . . *you're* still alive.'

'Yes, but it *is* dying. Slowly but surely. And it can't evolve a defence against what's killing it.'

'Why?' asked Paul. 'I thought it could protect itself against anything.'

'Yes, but . . .' Shelley groaned and slid slowly down the

wall until he was sitting on the floor. With an obvious effort
he spoke again. 'By over-dosing it with heroin you have made
it totally dependent on the drug. Now it is experiencing fatal
withdrawal symptoms. It can't evolve a defence against this
threat because it has become its *own* enemy. The Phoenix is
self-destructing . . . its own body is destroying it and it can't do
a thing about it . . .' He closed his eyes.

There was a period of silence until Paul said dubiously, 'I'd
like to believe that.'

'It's true. The only thing that will keep the creature alive is
another dose of heroin.' He opened his eyes. 'There's none
left, is there?'

'No,' said Linda quickly. Shelley might be telling the truth
– she was more than half-convinced herself – but if he wasn't
it would be stupid to let the thing know about the rest of the
heroin that Paul was carrying. And besides, if this was Shelley
he was probably feeling in urgent need of a fix himself. He
was, after all, sharing the same body as the thing.

Paul backed her up. 'We used it all. Your creature would
have to travel a long, *long* way to reach another supply.'

'Good,' sighed Shelley. 'Then it's definitely over. We will
have destroyed this monstrosity that we so foolishly brought
into the world.' A violent shudder ran through his body and
for a second or two his face seemed to shimmer out of focus.
Then he was back. 'Won't be much longer,' he said weakly.
'It's beginning to break down inside.'

'How much longer before you . . . you . . . ?' asked Paul.

A flicker of a smile appeared on Shelley's lips. 'Die? Possibly
only minutes. But don't be sorry for me. I look forward to the
release that death will bring. At least I didn't suffer the fate of
my friends and colleagues . . . I have stayed myself to the end.
I wasn't . . . *taken* . . . by that horror. I only lost my body . . . not
my soul . . .'

'There's one more question,' said Paul urgently. 'You've got
to tell us – is there only *one* creature?'

Shelley gave a feeble nod. 'Yes. Only one. It didn't need to reproduce. It didn't even possess the capacity for reproduction, either asexually or bisexually . . .'

'I don't follow you,' said Paul. 'Why couldn't it reproduce?'

'I told you – it didn't *need* to reproduce. Species only reproduce in order for their genes to survive, or we could say that genes themselves have contrived for the species to reproduce in order to improve the chances of their own survival. But because the Phoenix organism is in itself immortal, or thought it was, it didn't have to rely on such a clumsy mechanism . . .'

'The Selfish Gene,' murmured Paul.

Another ghost of a smile from Shelley. 'Ah, I see you have seen my video tapes. Young man, you must ensure that those tapes are seen by the right people. Steps must be taken to ensure that something like the Phoenix can never be unleashed upon the world again. Do you promise?'

Paul nodded. 'Don't worry. We'll make sure the full story of what happened here gets out.'

'Good,' said Shelley. He gave a deep sigh and his head lolled back on his shoulders. His features began to melt and run together. Then there was a hissing sound and something black emerged from between his lips.

'Get back!' Paul warned Linda. They began to retrace their steps up the corridor, keeping the lamp trained on the squirming shape on the floor. It was then that Linda realised they'd left the flame-thrower up on the landing pad.

Shelley rapidly disappeared and in his place was the familiar horror of the pool of glistening black slime. But it was different this time. Its viscous surface was rippling and bubbling in an agitated manner. Then thick, greasy-looking fumes began to rise up from the liquid.

Both Paul and Linda started to cough as the acrid gas reached them and were forced to back even further away. 'What's happening to it?' wheezed Linda.

'It's dying – I *hope*,' said Paul.

They watched it for about ten minutes. By the end of that time there was nothing left of the creature but a scattering of dried, black flakes. Eventually Paul walked carefully towards them and then prodded through them with the barrel of the M16. 'Careful,' warned Linda.

'It's okay. There's nothing left but ashes. It's all dried up. It's dead.'

'But how can we be *sure*?' She wanted to believe it was dead, with every fibre of her being, but the suspicion remained. The thing had tricked them before.

'We can't be. Not absolutely,' said Paul. 'But I'm 99% convinced and that's good enough for me.' He came back to her, a wide grin on his face. 'I really believe it's all over.'

'God, I hope you're right. But what do we do now?'

'We find that other pilot,' said Paul, slinging the M16 over his shoulder. He sounded almost carefree and she half-expected him to start whistling at any moment.

'How do we know he's not in *there*?' she gestured at the pile of blackened flakes. 'The thing might have got him while we were up top.'

'No, I don't think so. In the condition it was in I doubt if it was capable of attacking anyone. I'm sure we'll find him safe and sound. Come on, let's go.' He set off down the corridor with a definite air of jauntiness.

Linda followed him wishing she could feel as cheerful as he obviously felt but she couldn't shake off the strong suspicion that their troubles were far from over.

Seventeen

They eventually found him outside. They were about to descend the gangway to the lowest level when he suddenly came running up the gangway towards them. He stopped when he saw them. He was a heavily built man in his late twenties. He had a crew-cut and was dressed in the same sort of overalls as the one Paul had shot.

He stopped when he saw them. 'Who the hell are you?' he

shouted. Linda noted the alarm in his eyes. He looked as if he had just received a bad shock.

'I'm Paul Latham. This is Linda Warner. Our yacht sunk and we ended up here a few days ago.'

'What the hell is going on around here? Where is everybody?' He spoke with a pronounced American accent.

'It's a long story,' said Paul. 'Just believe me when I say there's no one left alive here but us and that we should get away from here as soon as possible.'

The pilot narrowed his eyes. He was looking at the M16 slung over Paul's shoulder. 'If you're the only ones here that means *you* shot Mike . . .' He reached down quickly and Linda noticed for the first time that he was wearing a holster.

But as he unbuttoned the flap and started to draw out a .45 automatic, Paul moved faster. He had the barrel of the M16 pointing at the man before the hand gun was even clear of the holster. 'Don't!' cried Paul. 'Drop your gun over the side.'

The man hesitated, obviously considering his chances of getting a shot at Paul before he could fire. Then, with an expression of disgust, he held the automatic out to one side and let go of it. It bounced off the gangway steps with a metallic clatter and disappeared. 'You *did* kill Mike, didn't you – you murdering bastard,' he snarled at Paul.

'It was . . . an accident,' said Paul helplessly.

'Yeah?' he sneered. 'Tell that to the judge. You're going to fry for this, kid. We got the death penalty back where I come from . . .'

Oh great, thought Linda as her sense of despair returned with a rush. After all we've been through we end up being convicted of murder. And who was going to believe their version of events? There was no evidence to back them up except a lot of empty clothes and piles of ashes. Then she remembered the video tapes . . .

'Paul,' she said urgently, 'we should go and get Shelley's tapes. No one's going to believe all this otherwise.'

'Yes,' he said wearily, 'You're right. I should have thought of that myself.' Then to the pilot he said, 'Look, I did shoot your friend but it was an accident and I'm sorry. It's just that ... well, things have been pretty bad around here ...' He shook his head helplessly. 'I wish I could explain but it would take too long. And it would sound crazy, fantastic ... you're just going to have to accept my word for the time being that I had a good reason for thinking your friend was dangerous. But I'm *no* murderer!'

The pilot obviously decided to change his tactics. With a slyness he couldn't conceal he said, in a conciliatory tone, 'Okay, kid, I'll give you the benefit of the doubt for now, but let me go back to my chopper so I can radio for some help.'

'No,' said Paul quickly. 'You'll call no one. Not yet. First we've got to go and pick something up. And you're coming with us. I warn you if you do anything stupid I'm going to have to shoot. I'll try not to kill you but that's not easy to guarantee with one of these things.'

The pilot went pale. He raised his hands. 'Hey, keep cool. I won't try anything, I give you my word.'

'Good. Get moving then,' ordered Paul, gesturing with the gun, 'Back the way you came ...'

Even though she knew the creature was dead – or at least she was nearly certain of it – having to go inside the platform again was the most difficult thing she'd ever done in her life. Once again the feeling returned that she was *never* going to see the end of these damned corridors – that she would spend forever wandering through the maze.

Then, when they finally reached the video room, they had to spend a long time sorting through the tapes trying to find the right ones. With the power off there was no way they could check to make sure so they decided to take as many as possible, using Paul's shirt as a make-shift sack.

While all this was going on the pilot, who'd been forced to lie face down on the floor with his hands behind the back of his head, kept asking questions.

'Are you guys going to tell me what the fuck happened here?' was the first one.

'I told you,' said Paul, 'it's a long story and you probably wouldn't believe it. That's why we need these tapes. To prove it.'

'What happened to all the people that were here?'

'They got eaten, in a manner of speaking.'

'*What?* Are you crazy?'

'See, I told you you wouldn't believe me.' Paul was examining cassettes in the weak light from the single lamp, trying to recognise familiar code numbers. Fortunately some of the cassettes were still sitting on the console and, as he told Linda, he was confident that the vital tape – the one they'd looked at last with Shelley's description of what had happened – was among them.

'What ate them?' asked the pilot, after a long pause.

'That's the difficult bit,' Paul told him. 'It's to do with what those scientists were working on here. You know all about that, don't you? You must do otherwise you wouldn't be here.'

'I'm just a pilot. I don't know anything.'

'Don't give me that,' said Paul with a bitter laugh, 'you knew this place was housing a secret laboratory. You also knew what they were doing here was illegal.'

'Is that so?' said the pilot warily. 'So tell me, what happened? What did you find when you got here?'

'You can read about it in the newspapers,' said Paul, tying the corners of his shirt together. It held over twenty cassettes. 'That's it,' he said to Linda. 'Let's get out of here – for good.'

Linda experienced a tremendous feeling of relief as the helicopter lifted off from the pad. The emotion was so strong it was intoxicating. She wanted to cry and laugh simultaneously. At long last they were actually leaving the hateful place . . .

'I can't figure why you still won't let me call in,' said the pilot. 'They must be getting pretty anxious by now back at my base.'

'Let them,' said Paul. 'You aren't touching that radio.' He

was sitting beside him in the co-pilot's seat and had the barrel of the M16 pointing at the top of his head. Linda was sitting behind Paul. The cabin was quite spacious and could probably seat at least ten passengers without any difficulty.

'Yeah? What will you do if I *do* touch it? Shoot me?'

'Yes,' said Paul.

The pilot laughed. 'I really doubt that. You might have shot me while we were down on the platform but not up here. You *need* me now. Shoot me and this baby falls out of the sky.'

'No it won't. I know how to fly a helicopter.'

'You're bluffing.'

'Possibly. But can you take the chance?'

The pilot didn't answer. Nor did he make a move towards the radio.

'Any idea where you're going?' Paul asked him.

'Yeah. There's another Brinkstone platform less than thirty klicks from here due east.'

'A *real* oil platform or the cover for another one of Mr Brinkstone's unusual enterprises?'

'It's a bona-fide oil rig, pal. And we'll be there in about ten minutes.'

'No we won't,' said Paul. 'We're not handing ourselves over to your people just like that. We know too many embarrassing things about Brinkstone. Your boss isn't going to let us walk free to talk to the media if he can help it. More likely we'd just disappear . . .'

The pilot laughed. 'Hey, hold on now. We're an oil company, not the goddamn Mafia. You really think old man Brinkstone would have you killed? You're crazy . . .'

'Yeah? If you're all so innocent why were you carrying a gun? And why did you have such a well-armed team of guards on the platform back there?'

'Security precautions, that's all,' he said curtly.

'Huh,' grunted Paul. 'Well, we're taking security precautions of our own. You'll fly us directly to the mainland. You'll set us down in a field or something right near a town.'

The pilot glanced at him with surprise. 'The mainland? But that's over two hundred klicks away. I don't have enough fuel.'

'Show me your fuel gauge,' ordered Paul, pushing the barrel of the M16 lightly against the pilot's cheekbone.

After a pause he pointed at one of the dials on the instrument panel. Paul peered at it then said, 'You're carrying enough fuel to fly us six hundred kilometres. I told you I know about helicopters. You've got more than enough to get us all the way to Aberdeen. So that's where we're going. Get your charts out and prepare a course.' He nudged him again with the gun barrel.

'I still think you're bluffing,' he said, but he reached down to the chart case clipped to the side of his seat and did as Paul ordered. Then, as he plotted a new course, he said, 'What will you do after you land?'

'Organise a press conference somehow. Get these tapes seen by the right people. Make sure the full story comes out. And make sure that steps are taken to see that what happened back on that oil rig never happens again.'

'And *what* did happen? You can tell me now. We've got time.'

'The scientists working for your boss accidentally created a new kind of life form. A highly dangerous one. It was practically unkillable. It was only through sheer luck we got rid of it . . .'

The pilot laughed. '"Practically unkillable" but *you* managed to get rid of it? Doesn't sound very dangerous to me. What exactly *was* it?'

'Well . . .' Paul hesitated. 'Well, it was a creature that could change its shape. It was genetically engineered to adapt to anything that threatened its survival. At times it looked human, other times it was a pool of moving jelly . . .'

The pilot gave a snort of disbelief. 'You give that story to the media and they'll lock you up in an asylum. It sounds crazy.'

'Yeah, well, it doesn't matter if *you* believe me or not,' said Paul defensively.

'Oh, but I *do* believe you,' said the pilot, removing his helmet.

Linda screamed. Staring out at her from the back of his head was a round, fish-like eye.

Eighteen

'Shoot it, Paul!' screamed Linda. 'Kill it!'

'I wouldn't advise that,' said the 'pilot' quickly. 'It would be inconvenient for all of us. Before I could reform this machine might possibly go out of control and crash. I would survive, of course, but you two wouldn't. And I *do* know, Paul, that you were bluffing about being able to fly it. I know everything about you that your friends did . . .'

Paul's face twisted with indecision. He backed away from the pilot, flattening himself against the door, but kept the M16 pointing at his head. 'Jesus,' he cried, 'Shelley lied – there *were* more than one of you!'

'Shelley? When did you speak to him last?' asked the pilot in a conversational tone. His voice hadn't changed – if it wasn't for the third eye staring blankly out at her from the back of his head Linda could have convinced herself that it was all a terrible delusion.

'I asked when you last spoke to Shelley,' he repeated. He continued to face directly ahead, not looking at Paul and ignoring the gun barrel. Linda saw Paul's finger tightening on the trigger but still he didn't fire.

'Just before we met . . . *you*,' said Paul. 'He told us there was only one of you. That you couldn't reproduce because you didn't have to.'

The pilot chuckled. And for a moment sounded like Alex. Linda wanted to scream again – to launch herself at the thing and rip at it with her nails – but she could only sit frozen in her seat, transfixed by the single, staring, unfathomable eye.

'I'm afraid that wasn't Shelley. That was me. Or rather the *other* me. Shelley had remarkable will-power. He held out longer than all the rest but in the end he had to succumb to me. It was inevitable.'

'Then there are *lots* of you?' asked Linda fearfully.

'No. Not *yet*. There is just me now. What the other "I" told you, apparently, while imitating Shelley was the truth. Or *had* been the truth. I didn't possess the means to reproduce but once it became obvious that the heroin was killing me I was obliged to rapidly evolve some sort of reproductive mechanism. The result was crude, but, as you can see, effective.' Again there came the obscene chuckle. 'And in a sense *you* two are responsible for this new development in my life cycle.'

'You got to the pilot,' said Paul bitterly, 'took him over . . .'

'Not in the way you think,' said the creature. 'Otherwise nothing would have been solved. There would have been *two* of us dying of heroin withdrawal. Instead I injected him with a small collection of newly-formed cells – an embryo if you like, but one that contained all the information and memories of the parent organism. In other words, a miniature version of *me*.

'Once implanted within the host the embryo grew and spread at a remarkably fast rate, cannibalising the host's various organs as it went. The whole process only took twenty-seven minutes from start to finish, though it was a very long twenty-seven minutes for the host, I'm afraid . . .' Again the chuckle. 'Yes, from the host's point of view my reproductive method has its drawbacks. Extremely painful ones. As you yourselves will find out before this flight is over.'

'Us?' Paul couldn't keep the fear out of his voice. 'Why do you need to reproduce again? You're not dying now?'

'Ah, but there's still only *one* of me. I know now – or rather let's say "I" am now aware on the genetic level – that I must continue to reproduce to ensure my survival. As I told you, thanks to your very nearly successful efforts to destroy me I have evolved a step further. As will always be the case whenever you puny humans attempt to stop me.'

'But does it have to be *us?*' cried Linda desperately. 'Couldn't you just let us go?'

'Idiot,' said the creature blandly. 'Fear is making you irrational. Anyway it pleases me to have you two as the carriers of my seed. As the ones who almost killed me it is fitting you should assist me in the introduction of my kind to your world.'

'You mean you intend to keep on reproducing?' exclaimed Paul. 'What will happen when . . . ?'

'What always happens when a superior species confronts an inferior one. The superior one overwhelms and eradicates the inferior – and I am unquestionably superior. I possess the combined intelligence of many of your scientists as well as great strength and various other unique physical characteristics, as *you* well know. I am the *ultimate* survivor. The end product of evolution because I will always be one step ahead of any competitor. And soon there will be ten of me, then twenty, hundreds, then thousands. The human race will quickly collapse and its remnants will be acknowledging its new masters . . .'

'But does it *have* to be like that?' cried Linda. 'You said yourself you have the combined intelligence of many people. With such great intelligence why do you need to be our enemy? Shouldn't you be *beyond* such primitive emotions as the need for violence?'

The single eye regarded her unemotionally for a few moments, then the creature said, 'You're confusing intelligence with some hazy notion of moral superiority. Just because something is intelligent doesn't necessarily mean it has a well-developed empathy for other living creatures. That concept is a piece of wish-fulfillment created by the more idealistic among your race. But your human system of ethics is meaningless to me anyway. This intelligence I possess – a mental patchwork of the minds I have absorbed – is nothing but another survival tool to me. At the core I remain what I originally was before those scientists, in their egotistic way, took me from my natural world and carried out their experiments. I still have the same primal drives . . . the same appetites . . .'

As he'd been talking his voice had gradually changed,

becoming harsh and guttural. And now he was beginning to change physically too. The skin turned to an unpleasant greyish-white colour and the head became more elongated. Then, when it turned to look directly at Paul for the first time Linda saw that the pilot's face had disappeared. A round, glassy eye, like the one on the back of its head, was the dominant feature in its profile. That, and a protruding lower jaw from which a forest of triangular teeth jutted upwards.

'But no more talking,' it said, fixing its gaze on Paul, 'I have pleasured myself with you long enough. I estimate we will reach the mainland in forty-five minutes and by that time I want you both to have completed the gestation process . . .'

What happened next reminded Linda of a demonstration she'd once seen on TV of a briefcase designed to be thief-proof. When activated, the case had sprouted long telescopic poles designed to prevent the thief from carrying the case any distance. A similar manifestation was now occurring with the creature. Several long appendages erupted from its body, bursting out through the pilot's clothing, and began to grow at alarming speed. Two of them, coming out of the top of its shoulders, attached themselves to the ceiling of the cabin, presumably to brace the creature, while others fastened onto Paul and Linda.

Linda screamed as three of the slimy things, which had burst out of the creature's back, pinned her to her seat.

'Don't struggle!' warned the creature. 'Remain still and accept the inevitable. Your agony will not be in vain – it will be serving a great purpose . . .'

'You bastard!' yelled Paul. 'You *enjoy* causing pain – and that makes you more human than you think you are. Yes, fish-head, you've become *tainted* along the way . . . there's probably more of *Alex* in you now than you . . . Superior species, my arse, you're just like us, only more so.'

'Silence! And be still! This is the delicate part . . .'

Linda saw that something else was emerging from the creature towards Paul. A white, pulpy-looking tentacle. On its tip was a sharp, thorn-like point from which dripped globules of black slime. Paul increased his efforts to break free when he saw the thing snaking towards his bare stomach but he was held tight by four of the thick appendages.

Tainted! Alex! The two words blazed together in Linda's mind with a significance she didn't, at first, consciously grasp. Then she realised she was staring at Alex's money belt around Paul's waist and it all fell into place.

'We have more heroin!' she screamed. 'You can have it! All of it!'

The point of the tentacle stopped moving. It was only inches away from Paul's flesh. 'More heroin?' asked the creature. 'No. You are lying.'

'In the belt! Look for yourself. We didn't use it all!' she cried frantically.

'It is of no significance to me. I don't want it.'

'There's *lots* of it!' she persisted. 'And you can have it all. Think of it!'

'No!' yelled the creature with surprising vehemence. 'I don't *need* it!'

But already one of the appendages had released its grip on Paul's shoulder and was fumbling at the money belt. Small rudimentary fingers, like those of a thalidomide victim, reached into one of the pouches and produced several packets of heroin.

Linda knew then that her gamble was going to pay off. She had remembered that when women heroin addicts gave birth their babies were similarly addicted.

The creature, though 'new-born' was *still* an addict!

Other appendages had joined the first one at the belt. More packets of heroin were pulled out of the belt.

'No!' cried the creature. But it couldn't help itself. The appendages holding the packets started to withdraw back into the body, taking the heroin with them. And as the drug disappeared into the creature Linda immediately felt its grip on her relax. 'No . . .' it repeated, but in a much weaker voice.

A few seconds later it slumped sideways in its seat and the

other 'arms' began to retract. Suddenly Linda was free. She knew what she had to do . . .

Undoing her belt she stood up and leaned across the thing's right shoulder. As quickly as possible she released its own seat belt, praying that it wouldn't stir.

'What . . . ?' began Paul dazedly.

'Shhh. Get ready.'

Now she was stretching to reach the door handle. The effort caused a flare-up of pain in her broken left arm but she ignored it. Her fingers touched the handle. She undid the safety catch then turned it. Then she began to slide the door open.

Paul now saw what she was doing. Quickly he swung his legs up and planted his feet against the creature's side. As Linda got the door open he kicked out . . .

But the contact, together with the rush of cold air into the cabin, had the effect of rousing the thing out of its somnolent state. As its body slid sideways through the doorway it gave a bellow of rage and made a grab for the edges of the opening. To Linda's horror it succeeded in getting a grip and hung there . . .

Linda gave a wailing cry of despair when she saw this. It was going to beat them after all.

There was a deafening explosion. Paul had opened fire with the M16. As the bullets tore into it the thing's head erupted, gushing black slime . . . It was as if it had been hit with a large, black tomato. The creature screamed. For a long moment it hung on then, abruptly, it vanished. One second it was there, its bulk filling the doorway, and the next there was nothing to see but grey sky.

Paul let out a cry of triumph. 'Sonofabitch! We did it!'

But there was no time to celebrate. The helicopter gave a violent lurch and then started to go into a spin. Linda screamed with pain as she was flung off balance and fell hard onto her broken arm. She was only dimly aware of Paul grabbing at the controls in a desperate attempt to bring the machine out of its spin . . .

Finally he succeeded. The sickening motion ceased and the helicopter was again flying on an even keel. Linda dragged herself upright and looked around. There was nothing to see through either the windows or the open door but grey cloud.

'Paul, what are we going to do?' she cried. The mental image of them crashing into the sea flashed unwanted into her mind.

'Don't ask me,' he yelled over the noise of the engines. 'I'm out of my league already! Hey, try and close that door, will you?'

She managed to slide the door shut. 'Will you be able to land it okay?'

'Are you kidding? I don't even know what direction we're going in. And I pulled her out of that spin by pure fluke.'

Linda peered over his shoulder to look at the controls. She saw he was gripping two levers and had his right foot pressing on a floor pedal.

'The thing on the floor controls the tail rotor,' he explained. 'And that's the tricky bit. Or *one* of them. I think you can use it to turn with . . . but I'm not sure how and I don't want us to go into another spin.'

'I thought you knew the *basics* of flying a helicopter,' she cried accusingly.

'I do, sort of. I know if you push forward on this lever here we go down, and if I pull back on it we go up. It tilts the plane of the rotors. And if I push this other lever to the side, we fly sideways . . .'

'Oh, that's marvellous.' How ironic it would be, after overcoming probably the most dangerous creature ever to exist on Earth, to die in a silly helicopter crash.

'Hey, it's going to be okay. We'll get out of this somehow.'

'*Sure*. We can fly sideways until we run out of fuel. Perhaps by then we'll be over a mattress factory.' She felt light-headed. Despite the danger they were still in she was experiencing a vast sense of relief. *It* was gone . . .

'Do you think it's dead?' she asked suddenly.

'Not yet, probably. But I think it soon will be. That was a massive dose of heroin it gave itself. Not as much as we injected into the other one but I'm certain it will be enough to do the job. It's about 200 miles from land – it won't last long enough to reach another supply of the drug.'

'God, I hope so Paul. But what if that *wasn't* enough heroin to kill it? What if it does get to the mainland?'

He shrugged. 'It'll be the government's worry then. Out of our hands. We'll give them all the information we've got – the cassettes – and leave it up to them.'

'*If* we make it,' she said darkly.

They flew on in silence through the grey cloud. Then Paul said, 'I'm going to try to take us down underneath this cloud. Then we'll give your original idea a go.'

'*My* idea? Which one was that?'

'Finding another oil platform and ditching this thing near it. It has floats. Our chances will be better in the water than me trying to come down on hard ground.'

The plan almost worked. Paul succeeded in bringing the machine down below the cloud level and after a tense half hour's flying they sighted another oil platform ahead in the distance. For one awful moment, as it emerged out of the greyness, Linda thought it was the same one they'd been on but as they drew closer to it she could see it was definitely a different rig. Instead of having four separate legs it rested on a huge single concrete pillar.

Paul also managed to guide the helicopter fairly close to the rig, swooping low in a wide circle around it to ensure its occupants were aware of their arrival. Then, when he was certain they'd been spotted, Paul started his descent, aiming to set the machine in the water some sixty yards from the platform.

'Brace yourself,' he warned Linda when they were about thirty feet above the water. 'I'm going to cut the engines. It's the only way I can be sure of setting us down without possibly driving this thing straight under the waves. The rotors will keep turning and should let us down pretty gently but there's still going to be a hell of a bump . . .'

He cut the engines and the helicopter began to drop like an express elevator. It would have been a perfect three-point splash-down if a sudden gust of wind hadn't tipped the machine over, causing it to come down on its side.

At the moment of impact Linda received a violent blow on the head and lost consciousness as water began to rush into the cabin. The next thing she knew she was outside with Paul's arm supporting her. Somehow he had got her out of the helicopter.

Choking and spluttering she looked up and saw another helicopter hovering above them. A man was being lowered on a cable towards them . . .

Very soon he was in the water beside them and slipping a rubber brace under her arms. Then suddenly she was being winched upwards to safety. She felt numb, dazed. She stared down at the heads of Paul and her rescuer in the water almost disinterestedly. Then she noticed that there was no sign of their helicopter. It had obviously sunk.

A terrible thought occurred to her.

She didn't feel the strong hands that pulled her into the helicopter nor did she acknowledge the concerned questions of the three men in the cabin. She could only think of one thing.

And when she saw Paul being winched up out of the water empty-handed her fears were confirmed. They had lost the cassettes!

Without them as proof would anyone believe their story? And what if the creature was still alive and making its way towards the mainland? Without the cassettes as evidence they'd never be able to convince the authorities of the terrible danger it presented. No precautions would be taken against its possible infiltration . . . no one would be on the look-out for it. Its planned invasion of humanity would meet no opposition. It would be like a fox loose in a chicken yard, and it would spread . . .

Linda sat shivering on the cabin floor, oblivious of the heavy coat that someone had placed round her shoulders. She knew the nightmare hadn't ended, but only just begun.

Lightning Source UK Ltd.
Milton Keynes UK
UKHW040800040319
338417UK00001B/214/P